P R A I S E   F O R
I, Claudia

"Claudia Procula—wife of one of the most controversial figures in ancient history—comes alive to twenty-first-century readers in a groundbreaking novel by award-winning author Lin Wilder ... Deeply researched, masterfully written, and tremendously entertaining." **–TopShelf Reviews** (5 stars)

"A fresh, entertaining take on one of the lesser-known women of the Bible ... Wilder paints a vibrant portrait of biblical times in this enjoyable story." **–Book Life**

"For someone who is looking for a fantastic plot of the ancient world filled with suspense, romance, and history, this is definitely the book you want. Not only is this a well-researched book that allows the reader to actually feel as if they are walking the streets in Judea and living within this realm, it's also a book that does not avoid controversy. It simply is a plot so well-crafted that the controversy comes second to the characters you will never forget." **–Feathered Quill** (5 stars)

P R A I S E   F O R
Malthus Revisited

"A threat that most readers can see as a real possibility, considering how far science and technology have progressed ... coupled with down-to-earth characters ... has your heart racing right till the end. While overtly spiritual in its plot, even the most atheist person could come to enjoy this story because it is a masterful blend of science and religion. With horrifying villains and inspiring heroes plus a few characters who you are never quite sure of which side of the good versus evil fight they stand on, this story is well worth the read." –**Literary Titan** (5 stars)

"*The Cup of Wrath* by Lin Wilder is a dystopian novel that is the perfect example of a thriller and a mystery all rolled into one. This is the fourth novel in the series; however, I had no issues with catching up or finding my rhythm. The novel follows multiple storylines, but the author handles them with great care and artistry. Lin Wilder did an amazing job in showing different stories and making them all connect perfectly. Fast-paced and tremendously developed, the story is riveting. The novel has compelling characters, especially Lindsey and Morgan. These two women are depicted to be strong, emotional, both fighters and human. I enjoyed the fact that they were as close to reality as possible. They seemed to come to life on the pages and I thoroughly enjoyed their journey and their progress. And don't even start me on the end!!! This book is simply amazing."
–**Rabia Tanveer** Readers Favorite (5 stars)

MY
NAME
IS
SAUL

ALSO BY LIN WILDER

Finding the Narrow Path
The Fragrance Shed by a Violet
Do You Solemnly Swear?
A Price for Genius
Malthus Revisited: The Cup of Wrath
I, Claudia

MY
NAME
IS
SAUL

A Novel of the Ancient World

Lin Wilder

My Name Is Saul
A Novel of the Ancient World
Lin Wilder

Print ISBN: 978-1-948018-49-4
eBook ISBN: 978-1-948018-50-0

Wilder Books
An Imprint of Wyatt-MacKenzie

DEDICATION

To John

Indeed you love truth in the heart;
then in the secret of my heart, teach me wisdom.
Oh purify me and I shall be clean,
Oh wash me and I shall be whiter than snow.
—Psalm 51

I said, "I will acquire wisdom"; but it was beyond me.
What exists is far-reaching; it is deep, very deep:
who can find it out? I turned my thoughts toward
knowledge; I sought and pursued wisdom and reason,
and I recognized that wickedness is foolishness and
folly is madness.
—Ecclesiastes 7: 24–28

Wisdom is the effulgence of eternal light
The spotless mirror of the power of God
The image of goodness
She, who is one, can do all things,
Whilst herself perduring
From age to age she enters
Into holy souls to produce
Friends of God and prophets.
—Wisdom 25-28

FOREWORD

AURELIUS
Corinth, Greece

On this third day before the ides of June, 811 years following the founding of Rome, I, Aurelius Maximus, legionnaire of the Roman Empire, testify that the words you are about to read are those of Paul the Apostle. Although the script is clearly my own rather than his, the document was dictated to me during our teacher's last night on earth. Where I felt it necessary to do so, I have inserted my own commentary, merely to clarify sections that otherwise might seem out of place or confusing.

There are legitimate reasons that the followers of Paul might find the provenance of this document suspect. First, this letter is dated four weeks after Paul's second letter to Timothy, the last one that he would write. Just as significant, I am known only to my fellow Christians here in Corinth. The rest of my brothers and sisters in Christ, those of you whom I will never meet, must make your own decision as to the veracity of my testimony.

No one knew of the crippling arthritis in the fingers and hands of Paul; he kept it even from Luke, his best friend. But the pain and deformities in his fingers became so severe during the writing of that second letter to Timothy that he was forced to ask my help in constructing its final sentences. Paul's handwriting had become indecipherable—a magnificent irony, and one that could be concocted only by Our Lord.

I was a Roman centurion before my tribune assigned me the shameful and odious role of primary jailer for Paul of Tarsus at Rome's Mamertine Prison, during his last nineteen months on this earth. I write this foreword to explain to you very briefly how and why a Roman soldier assigned to guard one of the foremost enemies of Nero came to write his last letter. Or, more accurately, how our Lord, Our Savior, used this very humiliation to bring me to my knees through his servant, Paul the Apostle.

It was during Mercedonius—Leap Month—813 AUC, that I was transferred from the battlefront of the Judean Wars to guard duty at Mamertine Prison. It was an assignment customarily reserved for foreign mercenaries, hastily and poorly trained battle fodder, rather than native Roman legionnaires.

The suddenness of my demotion, followed by my return to a Rome I no longer recognized, nearly destroyed me. I had been a centurion since the age of twenty-two and had expected to live out my years as a warrior or die honorably on the battlefield.

Although it had been three years since the Great Fire, my native city remained shattered, ruined. Yes, of course, I knew about the week-long fire; we all did. And I thought I was prepared for its aftermath. But nothing could have girded me for such massive devastation.

This Rome was unrecognizable—nothing like the beautiful, vibrant, and cultured center of learning I had grown up in. Even after three years, most of its formerly magnificent temples remained in ruins; there had been no attempt to rebuild them. As I walked the streets, now populated by Idumeans, Hispanians,

Numidians, Franks, Syrians, Egyptians, and slavish people from all ends of the Empire, I seldom heard Latin spoken. These hordes teemed into the city for the free food, housing, and depraved entertainment provided by Nero as he fought to maintain control of the senate.

The reasons for my tribune's decision to send me on this mission are irrelevant to my purpose here; what matters is the fact that I craved a way to externalize my humiliation; to find someone worthy of my enmity. I discovered him in Paul the Apostle, enemy of the Empire.

My treatment of Paul during the first few weeks of my assignment was reprehensible. The iron chains I fashioned around his torso were unnecessarily constraining—at times, inhibiting his breathing and reopening poorly healed lashing scars. I delighted in inventive methods to provoke him and cause him pain. Frequently I taunted him by pouring his tiny portions of food and water onto the ground a tantalizing distance from his lips. Tormenting him with deprecations of his inane savior, Jesus, became a favorite activity.

After nine days of all but starvation and intense thirst, Paul spoke his first words to me—in calm, flawless Latin. "I wonder why such a fine-looking specimen of a man has come to *detest* himself to such a degree that he causes himself such agony?"

How can you ask such a thing? You, in chains, me, your captor?

Why does the look in your eyes make me want to drop to my knees and sob like a child of three years?

Why don't you hate me?

The strange light that emanated from his eyes had not diminished despite his emaciation and parched, cracked, and bleeding lips. In fact, the fire had intensified. And there was a quality about him that defied description ... a stillness having nothing to do with his chains. The man had an inner serenity that no execrable words or deeds of mine could disturb. When I finally looked into his eyes for the first time, instead of a mirror of my own rage and hatred, I saw what I could only interpret as love. For me.

How can this man look at me with the tenderness of a mother gazing upon her infant?

My jaw dropped open. I could not hide my amazement.

"Who are you?" I asked him. "Why don't you detest me, as I do you?"

"You do not detest me," he replied in a whisper—the most substantial voice he could manage to propel through his ravaged lips. I leaned down to hear him and found myself irresistibly drawn to this scarred shell of a man. "You hate yourself... what you have become," he continued, not without difficulty.

The light in his eyes seemed to blind me. I wanted to spit in his face, curse him for speaking this way to his captor, but it was as if I had been struck deaf and dumb. My knees folded as if a pair of giant hands had applied such force to my shoulders that I had no choice but to kneel on the dirt floor beside him. Now, I was so close that I could see the pores in his skin.

He said nothing—merely pinned me with his gaze. After what seemed like hours but was probably just a few minutes, he laughed, then coughed violently. "You should probably give me some water," he rasped.

Without a second thought, I jumped up, opened the door to his cell, and raced over to the enormous wooden barrel of water that sat outside the cells of the prisoners, but was meant for the guards. I grabbed a cup from the stack and filled it. Then I carried it back into Paul's cell, where I crouched down beside my prisoner and brought the full container to his lips. As he struggled to make contact with the rim by leaning forward the few inches permitted by the heavy irons, I said, "Wait! Let me unchain you." Unabashedly shirking my responsibility as his jailer, I carefully removed the chains around his chest and torso, feeling more excited than I had in many years.

Something is happening here. This man has wisdom and is willing to share it with me. I feel as if he can see into my soul!

Now you know how the process of my becoming a follower of the Way—becoming a Christian—began.

That Our Lord has trusted me with the task of recording the last words of the greatest man I have ever known, the prisoner who set me free, is a thing of such grandeur, splendor, and glory that I will spend all of my days attempting to prove myself worthy of His—and Paul's—trust.

To God be the glory.

Paul—previously known as Saul of Tarsus—began his story with the prologue you will shortly encounter because he wanted his readers to understand instantly that this last is unlike all the other letters he has written and distributed to Christians throughout our world. Perhaps more than many of us, Paul understood how readily we confer honor and respect upon men undeservedly. Profoundly aware of the awe he inspired in Corinth, Ephesus, and Antioch, Paul hoped that this last letter would convey his truth. It tells the tale of the worst, most vicious persecutor of Christ, a man who committed the most heinous acts against other men. If Saul of Tarsus, who struck abject terror into the hearts of the followers of Christ, can be reborn as Paul the Apostle and be used by Our Lord and Savior Jesus Christ to bring about His Kingdom here on earth, surely, you—a far less depraved sinner than he—can move mountains.

SAUL
Tarsus, Cilicia

"Saul. Where is Saul? Come out, come out! We need to see you!"

My sister Esther, thirteen when I was born, never tired of our games. And she could run like the wind, with Rachel, Anat, and Mikhal trailing behind her.

"Is that you?"

She was looking behind a sand dune at the beach, knowing full well I was not hiding there.

Louder, she called, "Saul! Where are you?"

The giggling of my sisters grew more and more breathless as they ran through the pure white sand and stood beside the dune that Esther had raced past ten minutes before, pretending she had not seen my tiny three-year-old self.

"I'm here, Esther! Here I am!"

"Saul, I was so worried!" With that, my tall, elegant sister plucked me off the beach to twirl and dance me across the sand. She tried and failed to keep her balance as our smaller sisters joined in the dance and finally, all five of us collapsed into the laughter that can only emanate from children: pure, musical, pristine. We were ready to return home to lunch and the loud complaints of our mother.

"Esther Mordecai House of Benjamin! Soon you will regret the towers of sand you bring into this house for your poor old mother to sweep up!" she'd shout. Sand ... always, it was about the sand. But Mother could not hide her smile or suppress the signs of mirth in her eyes.

That smile, that laughter would be extinguished in just nine years.

My name is Saul. In Hebrew, it means *asked for* ... *inquired by God ... great*. When my father gave me the name, he encumbered me with expectations. We are born of the tribe of Benjamin, one of the twelve tribes of Israel, and I am named after the youngest son of the patriarch Jacob and his wife Rachel ... and for Israel's first king, anointed by the Lord's prophet Samuel. Because we are Roman citizens, I was given a second name, but I will never use it: *Paul*.

At twelve, I was sent to the Jerusalem Temple to study the Tanakh under Gamaliel. This was a privilege offered to no other boy in Tarsus, and one that cost my father dearly, for I was his only son, the youngest of five.

In my dreams, I can sometimes hear the howls of my mother, as my father and I climb the steps of the carriage to make the six-week trek from Tarsus to Jerusalem. Her laments would not cease until her death six months later.

I knew not to cry. I worked to welcome the pain I felt as her wails faded into the distance. I watched my father's expressionless face as the snow-covered mountains of Tarsus disappeared behind us. I forced myself to block the happy childhood memories of being chased by my sisters through the lush southern meadows to the shores of the Mediterranean ... the sheer delight and joy of hiding and then being found.

As if reading my mind, Father frowned and began to

recite the first line of Psalm 18: "You have given me the shield of your salvation ..." This was the beginning of King David's songs that I had memorized at the age of six. My sad thoughts were banished by the power of David's words. Confidence returned as I joined Father in the recitation of a verse that enveloped my soul with faith, trust, and delight:

Your right-hand holds me up;
by answering me, you give me greatness.
You have stretched the length of my stride,
my feet do not weaken.
I pursue my enemies and surround them;
I do not turn back until they are no more.
I smash them to pieces, they cannot stand,
they fall beneath my feet.
You have wrapped me round with strength for war,
and made my attackers fall under me.
You turned my enemies' backs on me,
you destroyed those who hated me.
They cried out, but there was no-one to save them;
they cried to the Lord, but he did not hear.
I have ground them up until they are dust in the wind,
trodden them down like the mud of the street.
You have delivered me from the murmurings of the people
and placed me at the head of the nations ....

It was on that journey that my father told me of his promise to God; of his petitions to Yahweh with the birth of each of my sisters: "Lord God of Israel, hear this son of Abraham, Jacob, and Ezekiel. If you would grant me a son, he should be consecrated to you in the Temple. I do not know of what these children come or how they are fashioned in the womb. Only this do I know: that You are the Most High, deserving of All Praise." Tears fell down his weathered cheeks and disappeared into his beard, once so black and now white with age. Never before had I seen my father cry.

Now, at the age of twenty-eight, occasional memories of what that small boy felt as he left the loving embrace of his mother return. For just a moment, weakened by sentiment, I let myself remember the softness of my young wife Hannah's lips, breasts, and touch. The sound of baby David's contented sighs as he nursed at her bosom come back to haunt me.

But then I regain control of my wandering thoughts. I cast such foolish and self-indulgent memories at the feet of the Name Above Every Other, the God of Abraham, Isaac, and Jacob.

The High Priest and the Council of Sanhedrins have given me letters empowering me to enter the houses of believers and arrest them. They know these people are worse than fools, these ignorant followers of the man called Jesus—a powerless carpenter from Nazareth who permitted himself to suffer the death of a criminal, crucified on a Roman cross. They claim that he is the Messiah, but he is merely another on the long list of fakers.

The time I was born for is here. I will wage war against these Christians, and I will emerge victorious.

My name is Saul.

I

Mamertine Prison, Rome

I will die tomorrow. In the morning, around sunrise.

I would like to see the sun. I cannot recall the last time I saw it, but I am confident that it has been at least a year and almost as many months.

About the death itself, am I afraid? Indeed, I am. I must confess that I fear the sight of the blade coming at my neck—for even Nero will not crucify a Roman citizen. During moments of terror about my death, I take comfort in my weakness, for I know the Lord will conquer all. I know that he pities even me, with my pathetic crumbs of faith.

There are two things for which I am eminently grateful: That I have been permitted to have fought the good fight and finished the race marked out for me; and that I will not have to endure another winter in this place.

My writing reeds are no more than useless bits of straw now, but even this is a good thing because the joints of my fingers are so swollen and sore that the act of writing is close to excruciating. Just yesterday, Aurelius offered to bring me a new supply of reeds, even a bronze stylus and nib. This young man astounds me.

Aurelius is the same Roman soldier who meticulously encased me in irons when I arrived early last year, all the while accusing me of being a "hater of mankind" because I decried Nero's Bread-and-Circus abominations. Now, he has read every word I have put to papyrus. Once it became too dangerous for Luke to come to the prison to collect them, Aurelius took over and smuggled them out.

This young and idealistic warrior reminds me of myself at his age. Overflowing with passion, fervor, and certainty, Aurelius has become a secret disciple. It is he who persuaded me to dictate this last letter. The process will commence when he returns with the supplies.

For over three decades, I have written about the Christ—He whom I persecuted during my final period of certainty about everything but the Lord. Through his grace, I can smile at my previous ignorance cloaked with dogmatism, which began early in my boyhood and continued throughout my second decade. My lips do not curve upward from amusement, but derision. I smile at the knowledge I have been granted by those I once decried: the pagan Greeks. I smirk at the magnificence of my own arrogance and stupidity.

It is clear now that the habit of certainty yields just one result: hubris. The great playwrights—Sophocles, Euripides, and Aeschylus—revealed as much quite poignantly in their tragedies. I am thankful to Father for his insistence on a Greek tutor. Pylenor was exceptionally well equipped to deal with the only son of one of the wealthiest merchants in Tarsus.

Are you surprised that a Hebrew born of the tribe of Benjamin knows and speaks fondly of Greek literature? Or that a Pharisee would have been schooled in the accomplishments of pagans? Those concerns are understandable. I will deal with them now since Aurelius has just entered my cell. He is a splendid specimen of a man, this Roman soldier. His beautiful features are alight with the love of Christ. The eagerness with which he undertakes his task touches my heart, as does his insistence that

I spend this night recalling my early life in Tarsus and my rabbinic education in the Jerusalem Temple, at the feet of Gamaliel.

Speaking about these early years naturally evokes memories of the happiest time of my life: my marriage to Hannah at eighteen, our ten idyllic years together in Cilicia, the birth of our child, and my return to Jerusalem as a widower, frothing at the mouth for an enemy worthy of distracting me from my grief.

This is a very long story that has never been told and is bound to exhaust this night. This time, the curve of my lips is genuine. I contemplate the image of Aurelius sitting by my side, his young, strong legs crossed as he unfurls and balances the scroll on a large slab of marble laid across his lap. He appears oblivious to the danger awaiting him, as it has each time he has spirited away my letters. That danger will loom again when the sun rises.

The affection I feel for this young man who once believed himself to be my enemy clogs my throat. I cough several times and hope he does not see the tears standing in my eyes as I gaze at him. I feel nothing but love for the son the Lord has granted me for the last night of my life on this earth.

II

Tarsus, Cilicia

It was a glorious day, not too warm, the air dry and crisp. This was unusual for Tarsus, where it was often oppressive, thanks in equal parts to the coastal humidity and the pagan ways of its citizens. Hannah had insisted on rising early in spite of her advanced pregnancy with our second child. It was my birthday, and my wife had declared it a feast day—just like that first evening of our journey back to Cilicia, which we'd spent together at the tavern in Antioch—and had laden the dining table with three types of bread, lamb, figs, and dates, accompanied by our usual goat's milk. There was so much that we decided to invite four of our servants to join us, along with Hannah's parents, Shimon and Leah.

Hannah had offered to come to the market with me, but she'd looked tired; this pregnancy was hard on her. The dark shadows under her eyes were a constant. Our little David's energy was inexhaustible. The only time he was still was when he was asleep, and it took all the strength she had to care for him. So, I left them at home with my father and the servants.

Although I was barely thirty miles away when the earthquake struck, it took me close to ten hours to get back to our farm. Had I still been at the market, I would have been killed or maimed, along with the thousands of others.

Every vendor in the city had been displaying his or her wares proudly. The array of meats and vegetables had looked enticing indeed as I wandered through the crowded agora, but I had stayed only a few moments. I was propelled away by a sense of anxiety I did not understand—an awful foreboding that took over every cell of my body. I rode hard and fast until ... it began.

At first, there was an almost undetectable tremor, hardly a shiver of the ground beneath my galloping horse Karisma's hooves. It was slight enough that I had begun to think I had imagined it when a deafening roar coincided with the formation of a veritable precipice in our path. Karisma stopped so abruptly that I nearly flew over her head. When I'd righted myself, I sprang to the ground to stare down into the vast crevice that only moments earlier had been smooth pasture. Karisma's eyes were wide and rolling at the trembling aftershocks under our feet. Placing my hand on her heaving flank, I thought of the hundreds of clamoring vendors and haggling customers back at the agora in Tarsus. *No one in the crowded city could have lived through this cataclysm.*

And then ... exploding into my consciousness came *Hannah! David! Father! Shimon and Leah!* I had to get back home immediately. Considerable gaps had formed in the land; the bridge over Cydnus had vanished, and the usually sparkling, gurgling river had grown so muddy it looked almost black. Ominous. The current spilled over its banks, and I knew it was only a matter of time before the area around it flooded.

Astride my steadfast Karisma, I carefully picked my way over the ruined roads, past the bloated bodies of dead livestock. As I finally neared the vast expanse of our land, the panicked bleats of kids filled the air. It was spring, and many of our goats had given birth. The cries of these babies were so weak and pathetic that I wanted to close my ears against the sound. They would die if they could not find their mothers—but I could not stop to help. I had to get back home to Hannah. To my son and father.

What had been some of the most excellent pasturelands in all of Cilicia was now split by a veritable canyon. It took my horse and me close to another five hours to find a stable path to what had been our home. By then, I understood the impossibility that any of my dear ones had survived.

The clarity of my memory of these long-ago events—of my ruined life—was astonishing. Although I'd witnessed the cataclysm more than thirty years earlier, it was as if I were *there*. I could hear the raspy wheezing of my exhausted, severely dehydrated horse, sense the sheer will and steadfast loyalty that motivated each laborious step she took.

At thirty-five years, Karisma was eight years older than I. The heroic Andravida had been mine since I was five, and within the hour, she, too, would be dead.

I could feel the impossibly fast, thunderous beating of my heart, the tears pouring from my eyes as I sprang from Karisma for the last time and continued my futile race on foot. I could feel my muscles and tendons ripping as I got down on all fours to scrabble through the ruins of what had been our magnificent home. Ignoring the deepening lacerations in my hands and knees and blinking the soot from my eyes, I leveraged massive limestone pillars and plunged into the debris beneath.

Please, Lord, please, I beg you, please, I prayed silently, knowing my prayers were too late. No one could possibly have survived such utter destruction. I continued to plead anyway.

After many hours—I had no idea how many then, nor do I know now—I found Hannah and David together. My wife had shielded the three-year-old's tiny body, vainly hoping she could protect him from the dagger-like shards of the collapsed roof and toppling pillars of concrete. She had done her job well. While her own body was broken and battered, there was not a mark on the child. He looked as if he were sleeping, his long dark lashes overlapping the pale skin of his cheeks. *How often had I watched my boy sleeping peacefully in precisely this pose?*

Less than a meter away lay the crushed bodies of my father, Hannah's parents, and the servants. Everyone, and everything was gone.

"Naked came I out of my mother's womb, and naked shall I return there; the Lord has given, and the Lord has taken away; blessed be the name of the Lord."

Sobbing, wretching, sick unto death, I recited the words of Job. He was no longer an ancient archetype to me, but an ideal entity of anguish and pure wretchedness who inhabited every cell of my being. His words soured my stomach and seared my lips as they tumbled from my mouth.

"Should we accept only good from God and not accept evil?"

Oh, how my words and thoughts mirrored Job's; how I wished I had never been born; and how I cursed all the celebrations I'd indulged in at the birth of my first and only male child—just as Job had. I rolled crazily in the rubble and debris for hours, or was it days? How terribly desperately I hoped to be struck down, for I knew I could not continue living without my loved ones. Surely, God would take me! The mere act of breathing seemed a betrayal. *How could I exist for another moment?*

Job's words continued to drop from my lips.

"If my anguish were weighed, my full calamity laid on the scales, it would be heavier than the sand of the sea, for the arrows of the Almighty are within me; my spirit absorbs their poison; God's terrors are arrayed against me."

But live, I did.

My mouth was suddenly so parched that I could not swallow. I reached for some water, only to note Aurelius staring at me, transfixed, his dark eyes dilated. The young man's expression seemed a curious blend of horror and anger. The scroll had rolled off of his lap and onto the floor. Clearly, he had written no words for several minutes.

I shook my head to wrest myself from the memories. The grief I was experiencing felt brand new; its coils tightened around my insides until I was almost panting. My face was soaking wet with the tears I'd imagined were memories. Even still, I could smell it ... the awful fragrance of death.

"What?" It came out sounding like a rebuke, which I did not intend. I'd only meant to rouse Aurelius, who continued gazing at me wide-eyed as if he had seen a ghost. And, of course, he had.

III

Mamertine Prison, Rome

"You are surprised that I was married, had a wife and children,"
I said to Aurelius, mitigating his shock or perhaps even rage.
Clearly, I had toppled from the pedestal he had constructed for
me and shattered into thousands of bits, maybe never to be
reassembled.

> *Good. Learn it now, my son. When you gain a friend,
> first test him, and be not too ready to trust him. For one
> sort of friend is a friend when it suits him, but he will
> not be with you in time of distress. Another is a friend
> who becomes an enemy and tells of the quarrel to your
> shame. Another is a friend, a boon companion, who will
> not be with you when sorrow comes. When things go
> well, he is your other self, and lords it over your servants;
> But if you are brought low, he turns against you and
> avoids meeting you. Keep away from your enemies; be
> on your guard with your friends. A faithful friend is a
> sturdy shelter; he who finds one finds a treasure. A faith-
> ful friend is beyond price, no sum can balance his worth.
> A faithful friend is a life-saving remedy, such as he who
> fears God finds; For he who fears God behaves accord-
> ingly, and his friend will be like himself.*

Ben Sira's *Book of Wisdom* was one of the first that Gamaliel had instructed his students to memorize. That passage on friendship had saved me on countless occasions. What Aurelius could not know was that I myself was a "life-saving remedy." Perhaps he would come to know this, but now he was filled with outrage that once I had lived an ordinary life—one without shipwrecks or torture. I had known the love of a woman and felt wonder at the birth of my son.

Aurelius nodded. He wet his lips, started to speak, then swallowed his words with a gulp.

I watched him, understanding. I could read his thoughts, and they pierced my heart. His olive skin was flushed as if from heat, though it was cold where we sat. It was always cold in this place. The young soldier met my gaze, then quickly averted his and stared at the concrete floor of the cell as if there were answers hidden there.

"You think His disciples should or must be virgins, is that it? That none of us should consent to sexual release and the love of a woman? To show Him love, we must be wholly miserable, I suppose … depriving ourselves of all comfort?"

Cheeks now flaming, Aurelius finally exploded, "I thought we had to leave family—everything—to follow Him. I thought that having wives and children was too …" He paused, searching for the right word.

"Pleasurable?" I interjected. "Satisfying? Joyous?"

The tears that had been looming now spilled over his features.

Lord, this young Roman soldier is me … so many years ago—except for that handsome face, that perfect form. I was never even slightly attractive. How my beautiful Hannah had loved such an unappealing visage as my own remains a mystery even now. She claimed even to love my bowed legs!

I spoke the words Aurelius could not. "Indeed, it is the

sacrifice we seek, the pain and valor, the mutilation … the lure is irresistible."

I knew that Aurelius had just recently insisted on circumcision, despite what I had taught him. Luke had explained to me that my young protegee had begged him for the mark that Christ bore. That Paul bore. On his knees outside the prison, Aurelius had pleaded with Luke to perform the procedure, and that dear and merciful physician could not refuse him.

"Paul, how could I refuse a request like that?" he'd exhorted me. "Even you could not have said no to this fervent brother, even you! But you must not tell him that you know!"

I had not. But now Aurelius suspected as much.

"Are you mocking me?" he asked, his eyes still wet. I could see the tumult in his expression as if he were a wounded child.

"No, my son, never would I jeer at you."

How can I explain in words what it had taken me more than thirty years to learn? That nothing we can undergo, no amount of sacrifice or torture, can alter the truth. This God-man born to die … we can give nothing to Him. We cannot earn what He has freely offered to all of humanity … each person who has ever walked the face of the earth and will until the end of time. There is no longer Jew or Greek, there is no longer slave or free, there is no longer male or female. All of us are one in Christ Jesus.

Who can grasp such impossible, unmerited love?

Looking over at the scroll that Aurelius had repositioned in front of himself so that he might continue setting down my story, I saw that he had recorded just two paragraphs so far. Most of my journey back in time to my beloved Hannah would remain untold. So be it.

IV

Tarsus, Cilicia

My mother was forty-five when I was born. By then, my parents had long ago surrendered any hope of having a boy. While Mother showered my four older sisters with love and attention, my father buried his disappointment at the lack of a son in his textile business. By the time I was born, Father had created one of the most prosperous textile companies in Tarsus. Our herds of goats, so prized for their hair and what could be fashioned from it, numbered in the tens of thousands.

Father was a respected and influential merchant. The Roman governor, Tacitus, was a personal friend and frequently consulted him on matters of State. Although our family was of the tribe of Benjamin, Father had many Greek friends, both in the Academy and proprietors of successful businessmen in the city. This fact would have a significant impact on the education of his only son.

My birth was cause for extended festivities. My oldest sister, Esther, claims she told me the story of the week-long celebration thousands of times, but Esther is prone to exaggeration.

As her story goes, I was just eight days old when much of the local population journeyed southeast to the Cilician plains to join in the week-long feast for the birth and circumcision of baby Saul. *Much of the population* was probably one of Esther's exaggerations, of course; the inhabitants of Tarsus numbered many thousands, and surely most of them had better things to do. Then again, it was an opportunity for the Jewish and Gentile merchants of the area to spend time socializing and planning business ventures. So, perhaps Esther was right about the attendance at my *brit milah*. We Jews enjoy celebrating new life, especially infant males destined for the rabbinate, as I was.

Jews were a minority in Tarsus, comprising less than one percent of the population of nearly a million souls. Only in reflecting back on my early boyhood do I see how my father had been compelled to straddle our exclusively Jewish world at home and the pagan one in which his business flourished. Only now is the providential nature of the rescue of his insatiably curious little boy made clear to me.

I was just four when I was chased by a group of boys far older than I. Even at that age, my Jewishness was evident from my dark complexion; large, prominent nose; and the dark brown, curly hair that mother refused to shear. The combination was a veritable red flag to the ruffians wandering the city in hopes of finding mischief.

I happened to be on the outskirts of the city when they spotted me, having run fast and far with no destination in mind, and was totally lost. At first, the four walked on by me. But the tallest and stoutest then turned back to shout something. Already I could speak rudimentary Greek, so I was puzzled that I did not understand the epithet. I realize now that Father's tutor would never have taught me the meaning of the odious phrase.

Momentarily bewildered, I stood still, waiting and curious, staring at their faces. Then I sensed the menace; the unspeakable hatred. Just as the closest one reached out to grab me, I took off and ran faster than I had ever run in my life, fueled by the fear of what I had not previously known existed in the hearts of anyone—let alone boys.

I wonder still what might have happened had a merchant not stepped outside to take in his produce for the day. Grasping the scene immediately, he grabbed me and shoved me behind him. Standing up to my would-be assailants, he inquired calmly, "Have you nothing better to do with your time than persecute a little boy?"

The youngsters looked far less dangerous now. Unable to meet the man's gaze, they shifted uncomfortably from one foot to the other. The shopkeeper called each one of them by name in turn, then asked, "Do your fathers know that this is how you spend your time? Shall I speak with them about this when I see them at the agora in three days?"

All four commenced begging him plaintively not to inform their fathers.

Once again curious, I tried to step apart to get a better view of them, but the man's gentle touch upon my shoulder turned rigid. It felt to me as if he wielded the hand of God.

The youths fled quickly, and all went quiet. Only then did my savior turn around slowly and crouch down to meet my gaze. "I think your mother and father must be anxious about you," he said, his face kind. From his appearance, he could have been a father to any one of the boys he'd chastised, sporting the same light hair and skin tone. Speaking slowly and enunciating clearly so that I could follow his Greek, he continued, "Can you tell me where you live so that I can make certain you get there safely?"

When I answered in passable Greek, he broke into a bright, broad smile.

The man walked beside me all the way back to our farm, asking me simple questions about my family as we traveled. Just as we turned onto the path that led to our courtyard, my mother exploded out of the house as if propelled by some unseen force. Esther, Rachel, Anat, and Mikhal followed, shouting my name. As Mother overtook me, she grabbed my right arm and began to shake me in anger and frustration. Father appeared from another direction, plucked me from her grasp, and swung me up to his shoulders. After whispering something to Mother I could not hear, he turned to the Greek and chuckled. "Demetrius! I know you could not possibly have recognized Saul from his *brit milah* some four years ago. How did you know that this little wanderer belonged here?"

"David," the Greek responded, "your Saul is an impressive little man." He patted me on the shoulder as he recounted the events that had taken place outside his shop and the fact that I'd provided accurate directions home.

By this point, Mother had calmed down. She persuaded my savior to join us for dinner.

Father and Demetrius conducted some business while Mother and my sisters got the meal on the table. Once we'd all eaten our fill, Father nodded at Demetrius, who, in turn, looked at me and smiled. "Saul," he said, "I understand that your fifth birthday is coming up and that you have been asking for a horse."

He paused as my eyes widened, and I nodded my head even faster than my heart was beating.

"That is very good because I have a twelve-year-old Andravida mare who needs a new home. The other horses persist in nipping and biting her, and I need someone who can give her a lot of love and attention. Could you possibly be that person?"

So excited I could barely speak, I squeaked out an eager *yes* and looked at my parents. Both were smiling.

"That is excellent news," said Demetrius grinning. "I will ask one of my servants to bring her to you next week."

It is odd that I have not thought about that incident for many years—the malicious intent of those boys just because I looked different from them, followed by the loving care and generosity of the Greek businessman who gave me my precious

Karisma. My still-innocent soul was, of course, wholly ignorant of the destruction I would shower upon other innocents before fifteen years had passed—simply because of their difference from me.

V

I loved learning, most probably because I excelled at the study of the Torah and languages. I could read or hear something just once and commit it to memory almost word for word. But, after the event with the Greek bullies, I withdrew. Whereas before I had been an open, outgoing, and inquisitive child, suddenly, I was quiet—almost shy. I grew unwilling to run across the beach playing hide-and-seek with my sisters. I even lost my appetite for my mother's cooking. As a consequence, my layers of baby fat evaporated, and I grew thin. I spent most of my time outdoors with Karisma, preferring her silence and gentleness to any of the childish games I had played before.

The solitude provided an ideal opportunity for me to ponder the remarkable influence of language upon one's thinking about people, ideas, and the world. I was becoming proficient in Latin and Greek, in addition to Aramaic and Hebrew—the languages of the Jews. Both Aramaic and Hebrew were fundamental for most of us because much of the Talmud was written in Aramaic, and Hebrew was the language we spoke at home. Since their alphabets are similar, it doesn't take long to attain fluency in both.

For my father and, presumably, his father before him, fluency in Latin and Greek was a business necessity. Father spoke both languages flawlessly, though I have no idea if he ever contemplated the impact this had on his worldview. Sadly, we did not discuss such matters. But Father did acknowledge that I needed these languages for Temple study, so he made sure they were part of my early education. My first tutors were tasked with teaching me the basics of writing and speaking both languages, starting with Latin. This I learned through mastering the *Iliad* and *Odyssey* of Homer, books I found challenging, but that failed to penetrate past the realm of the intellect. The reason for this, I think, is that they focus on the existence of multiple gods I knew to be powerless, if not imaginary.

But, when Pylenor introduced me to Zeno and his philosophy of Stoicism, I was shaken from my fear-filled torpor. Father had increased Pylenor's tutoring time from half a day to two days per week so that I could become fluent in Greek. A kind and wise man, Pylenor observed a spirited response from me as he unspooled the narratives of Sparta, King Leonidas, and the Battle at Thermopylae. I took to these tales as if born for the task, asking for scrolls of my own so that I could read Herodotus and Thucydides. When Father noticed the improvement in my Greek, he elevated Pylenor to fulltime tutor, overseeing all but my training in the Torah.

"What do you see as the main distinctions between Latin and Greek, Saul?" Pylenor asked me as we sat studying in the courtyard. As usual, he had brought a bundle of scrolls for us to study together, and they were arrayed about us.

I stared at him, and, for some reason, my thoughts turned to Demetrius and his gift of Karisma several months earlier. "Latin is more analytical," I answered, touching my forehead, "while Greek feels similar to Hebrew."

Pylenor raised his eyebrows in surprise. "Why do you say that?" he asked.

In response, I picked up one of the scrolls of *The Odyssey*, which we had been studying for several weeks.

"Although we learn much about the obstacles Odysseus faces, we know almost nothing about his perception of what is happening to him," I said. "We are never told about his thoughts or feelings. It's an account—kind of like reading Herodotus—whereas the Greek plays of Sophocles are crammed with details about how the main characters feel, what their thoughts and fears are. Oedipus and the rest become real to us because they invite us into their hearts. Like Hebrew, Greek is an emotional language—a language of the heart. Latin, not as much."

Father traveled extensively throughout the region and was frequently away for weeks at a time. At six, I was still too young to accompany him, but not to begin learning a trade as well as the Torah. I became an apprentice in one of his shops, where the hair from our goats was made into tents. It was there that I commenced my studies with Shimon ben Hur—my first teacher of the Law after Father.

While Father was in perpetual motion, verbally and physically, Shimon was still. Even while moving from one area to another within the large warehouse where the cilicium tents were constructed, he glided rather than walked. Shimon was a striking man, tall and lean even in the sixth decade of his life. He drew smiles as he stopped to suggest a remedy for the bleeding hand of a new worker, or crouched beside another to show him how to reinforce the seams of a tent. I ran ceaselessly to keep up with him.

Shimon was a partner, an accountant in Father's business as well as a mentor to my family. Since both my parents were only children, Simon and his wife Leah functioned as uncle and aunt to my sisters and me. Shimon's love for the Torah and the prophets would be equaled in my experience only by that of Gamaliel, but I was far too young to understand the gift of a man like this—a truly righteous man.

Each jot and letter of the law was beloved to Shimon; the words of Jeremiah and Isaiah were so familiar that passages flowed naturally from his lips when they were most needed. Vastly more powerful than these intellectual gifts, however, were his innate discretion, sensitivity, and wisdom—qualities I would not appreciate until much later in my life.

There was the time I humiliated myself, Father, and a whole hoard of family friends by forgetting that the evening Shema is preceded by one benediction and followed by two. Since my seventh birthday fell on a Friday, Father had asked that I lead the evening prayers at the synagogue. To this day, I can picture the expression on his face—indignity, and scorn at my gaffe warring with forbearance and equanimity. In the end, scorn triumphed. And I can hear the gasp of my sisters and mother from the women's section to the right and above where I stood.

Father had had no reason for concern when he'd asked Rabbi Eliezer to permit my participation at an evening service on that Friday in June. After all, I had been reciting the Shema and leading my family in weekday prayers since I was five years old. My stomach grumbled over the entire mile-long walk to the synagogue. Evening Shema was not offered until three stars could be seen in the sky, and we did not eat until afterward. Mother had set the table for Shabbat before we left. I'd seen the challah sitting between the candles and smelled the fragrance of the lamb that permeated the house.

I was the first to arrive at the synagogue. Excited and proud, I ran up the seventy-seven stairs, through the arched lintel, and into the large rectangular chapel. Although I had run the nearly six meters from our home, I was barely breathless. In the light of the setting sun, the white limestone of the holy structure was cast in a divine light. I had been *chosen*.

Moving quickly through the door of the inner Temple, I

was then slowed by the crowd of people standing and murmuring. The thought that I faced Jerusalem never ceased to thrill me, but tonight even more so. I knew that the synagogue was a facsimile of the Jerusalem Temple: A place as close to heaven as anyone could ever reach.

I forgot my hunger as I moved toward the *bima*—the platform upon which I would stand and lead the congregation in prayer. Behind the *bima*, along the rear wall of the building, the ark containing the sacred scrolls sat behind a scarlet veil. I, Saul, would stand in front of the Holy of Holies to proclaim the Shema!

My heart was hammering, not in fear but in anticipation. I felt jittery, as if about to compete in a race. At the signal from Rabbi Eliezer, I began.

I covered my face with my right hand and prayed from memory, beginning with the beautiful Berakhah One and Two—the Creation and Revelation blessings—then moving on to the Shema, and ending with the Berakhah Three: God Alone is the Eternal Redeemer.

Although the synagogue was very full that night, the solemn faces of the men in front of me faded away once I began my recitation. I was caught up in the beauty of the words, the worship, and did not notice the occasional appreciative mutter as my vigorous young voice proclaimed the majesty of God.

Hear, O Israel, the Lord is our God, the Lord is One.
Blessed is the Name of His glorious kingdom for all eternity.

You shall love the Lord your God, with all your heart, with all your soul, and with all your resources. Let these matters that I command you today be upon your heart. Teach them thoroughly to your children and speak of them while you sit in your home, while you walk on the way, when you retire, and when you arise. Bind them as

*a sign upon your arm and let them be tefillin between
your eyes. And write them on the doorposts of your
house and upon your gates.*

*And it will come to pass that if you continually hearken
to My mitzvot that I command you today, to love the
Lord your God and to serve Him with all your heart
and with all your soul—then I will provide rain for your
land in its proper time, the early and late rains, that you
may gather in your grain, your wine, and your oil. I will
provide grass in your field for your cattle and you will
eat and be satisfied ....*

Upon my flawless completion of the Shema, I stood
silent, eyes closed, lost in the majesty of the prayer. After a few
moments of silence, I heard the Rabbi chant:

*Your teaching is true and enduring. Your words are
established forever. Awesome and revered are they, eter-
nally right; well-ordered are they, always acceptable.
They are sweet and pleasant and precious, good and
beautiful and beloved ....*

Only then did I understand that I had omitted **Blessing
Three, God Alone is the Eternal Redeemer.**

Startled and somewhat dazed, I opened my eyes to find
Father staring at me, his thick, black-and-white eyebrows—so
like my own—drawn together and his lips pulled down in a
frown. His black eyes were cold and distant. I knew that look.

Paralyzed with shame, I did not know who swept me
off my feet until I heard Shimon whisper, "Before I formed you
in the womb, I knew you, and before you were born, I consecrated
you: I appointed you a prophet to the nations."

Shimon.

VI

The walk home was cold. Joyless. No one dared speak.

Mother's irresistible Shabbat dinner was consumed by the servants. I could hear Shimon speaking softly with Father, and I knew he was trying to intercede on my behalf. I also knew that his importuning would have no effect on Father. Or, for that matter, on me.

Shimon's lovely daughter Hannah tried to hold my hand, as we had done so many times in the past, but I shook her off. I was already filled with the righteous indignation that would nearly extinguish my soul. Bitterly, I recited the first few lines of the Prophet's song:

> *I trusted, even when I said:*
> *'I am sorely afflicted,'*
> *and when I said in my alarm:*
> *'No man can be trusted.'*

I paid no attention to the expression on Hannah's beautiful face or the tears slowly making their way down her cheeks. I ignored her hand, still dangling in the air with fingers spread apart like the starfish we would find on the beach and return to the ocean. I was too busy making promises to myself. Promises I would keep.

Fiercely, I vowed to become known as the Guardian of the Law. Even in Jerusalem, I would be famous for my mastery of the Torah, the Nevi'im, and the Kesuvim. All twenty-four books of the sacred scrolls of Moses, the prophets, and the Writings would be as familiar to me as the face of my mother.

Never again will I err in the recitation of the Shema. Never will I err on any of the Laws or of any portion of the Torah. Never will I omit a prayer or phrase. Starting now, I will be known as the most zealous of any Jew who ever lived. I will see each jot of our 613 laws as clearly as the hand in front of my face. Better than any man before me, will I follow the Law. Others will tremble at the power of my comprehension.

Of course, I was wholly ignorant of the cost of such audacious pretension—to myself and to so many innocents.

VII

Mamertine Prison, Rome

Abruptly, I ceased my dictation and pacing of the perimeter of my cell at Aurelius's cry, "Teacher, please! You must speak more slowly! I am fluent in Greek, but understand it is, after all, not my native language. Therefore, some of your terms are foreign to me. I must ponder their meaning by focusing on your context, but by then, you have moved on, and I must trust my recall ... " After a long exhalation, Aurelius took a deep breath, obviously working to calm himself. More quietly, he said, "These words are your last, so I must be precise. They must be the words of Paul, not Aurelius!"

I remained still, staring at him. His dark eyes were wide, brows drawn together in a frown which, as I stared, faded and began to turn to regret at offending me. His mouth formed a perfect O, but before he could take back his words, I said, "Aurelius, I apologize. I have immersed myself in my own life ... in the telling of it, trying to render the tale perfectly and never giving thought to how well you could keep up or even understand what I was saying ...."

Honestly, I was shocked at my own arrogant behavior. Heedless of the effort required by Aurelius to keep up with me, I had focused purely on myself. *Even now, when the end of the race is clearly visible, it takes mere seconds for Saul to appear. Saul, the Great One.*

I crouched down on my swollen, arthritic knees and rejoiced at the pain. Pain brought me back to my senses. Gently, I placed my hand on Aurelius's cheek and whispered, "My son, let us work together on the pages you have written. I am sorry that I have caused you such anxiety. It will not happen again, I assure you."

We spent more time than Aurelius had hoped would be necessary, laboriously reviewing what he had written to ensure its accuracy. Dawn would come in just under ten hours. Aurelius was right, of course; we had no time to waste.

But I knew that when we began again, we would be able to pick up speed. The time spent had been precious in teaching us both. I, who had never dictated before, now had a ready understanding of the pace at which I should speak, along with a new sensitivity to my scribe. I knew that Aurelius had been well educated before he'd entered the Legion, but I had not appreciated the scope of his learning until we had this discussion. Some of his editorial suggestions were exceptional in clarifying my intent. Although Greek was not his native language, his comprehension of it was excellent—almost as good as my own.

During our two hours of effort on the pages, we compared aspects of our early education and were surprised by the similarities. Aurelius's understanding of many of the Stoics was most comprehensive, and the vernacular of the observant Jew was not as alien to him as he had indicated when he spoke of racing to keep up with me. After my explanation of the Torah and daily prayers of the Jew, I watched him grow calmer. His posture changed, those exceptional features relaxed, and his innate confidence returned. Only a few of the Jewish expressions were foreign to him, and the majesty of the prayers was quickly assimilated by his gifted mind.

I found myself smiling, and that unfamiliar action in itself widened my sense of happiness. I could not recall the last time I had done this. Stunned and filled with awe, I wondered how it was possible that I could feel anything resembling joy at this moment. Had the terror at the thought of the executioner's blade disappeared? Was I anticipating seeing my Lord face to face? Assuming the radiance of Moses but without the veil?

My mind wandered back to Stephen: my best friend and confidant and a man I had loved as well and dearly as any on this earth. I braced myself for the terrible gnawing pain that had accompanied me almost unceasingly since the fateful day of his demise close to thirty years ago. That thorn clawed its way through muscle, bone, and sinew.

In spite of the advancing hour, I felt wholly confident that we'd have sufficient time to complete this task. We would finish. Apparently, Our Lord wanted this last letter from me, from Saul, who had been named after Saul the Great but who He had renamed Paul.

So be it.

I waited patiently while Aurelius copied all of the pages that required rewriting. The soldier sat cross-legged, head bent low as he worked. The scratching of his quill on the papyrus was almost soundless, but if I concentrated, I could hear the rhythmic, soothing *tick-tick-tick*.

VIII

AURELIUS

Corinth, Greece

Dear Reader, allow me, Aurelius, to interject here. I offer these few pages to provide some necessary clarity on all that has come before and all that follows.

Halfway through that last night of Paul's life, I realized that what I'd thought had been my own inspiration had not been mine at all. In fact, the whole endeavor had been orchestrated by Our Lord.

After close to two years of spending time with this remarkable prophet, I thought I understood him—that I grasped the essence of the man, his motives, and nature. Despite our glaring superficial differences, we were strangely similar. Like Paul, I had undergone a radical transformation. Like him, I had persecuted and tortured Christians—he, foremost among them—only to find that *I* had been the actual prisoner. I had learned that there were no irons strong enough to restrain this man, for there was scarcely anything left of him; he was filled with the Christ.

Having come to this realization, and having devoured his teaching, I wanted to do something for him in return for his gifts. I wanted, in some small way, to atone for my barbarous treatment of him, which had been motivated by a hatred whose source was fear. He had given me my very salvation, and I wanted to give him something back.

I was convinced that Paul had far more to say after his last letter to Timothy; far more to explain to all of us in danger of succumbing to the manifold lies of this world. Quite simply, I hoped to help the foremost Apostle of the Gentiles disseminate a few last words. I was his jailer; might I not also be his scribe? The idea was imbued with a certain irony that only the brightest of his disciples would pick up on. But, as you no doubt see clearly, it was I who received a final gift, not Paul, a gift I am honored to pass on to you and countless multitudes throughout the centuries.

Since any tale is most reasonably told chronologically, particularly a biographical one, I rearranged the sequence so that Paul's story might be absorbed in order. I began with his life as a small boy in Tarsus, moving on to his study in Jerusalem, and so forth. I labored to bring him to life on the page—but with each new iteration, Paul's words grew duller and lost most of their zest ... until finally, they seemed to lay lifeless on the scroll and on my lips. Only after completing my tenth or perhaps twelfth arduous revision—more than three weeks after Paul's death—would I realize that the story of his early life could not be conveyed linearly, sequentially.

Saul of Tarsus's unique journey from proud, feared, and zealous Jew to Apostle of the Gentiles and the foremost evangelist for the Jesus Christ he once persecuted, could not be fashioned conventionally or constrained by literary convention. To do justice to the man himself, this chronicle had to be conveyed as he recounted it to me—moving freely from a young man who lost his entire world to an elder within the span of a few paragraphs. In most of our lives, the past presages the future; the father shadows the son. But in this extraordinary life, the boy and husband Saul had to be fully integrated within the man Paul. The past and present had to coexist.

Upon this realization, I burned all of my laboriously edited and copied scrolls. What you are reading is the original story, related in the exact order in which Paul dictated it to me.

Speaking about one's life as it dwindles down to its final last twelve hours is an extraordinary task. Paul did so with detachment and eloquence. Initially, the shadow of his impending death—his knowledge of the precise number of hours he had left—seemed to encase him in a most understandable sense of anxiety. The urgency of getting so much expressed, understood, and recorded caused us both extreme apprehension. But when Paul became aware of the limitations of my comprehension, as well as my difficulty in keeping up with him, he experienced a type of epiphany. This happened just after he'd recalled the wholly reprehensible execution of his best friend, Stephen, and I found myself pleading with him to go more slowly. The change in Paul at that moment was tangible. As I watched in wonder, his crippled and deformed body and wasted facial features transformed to wholly perfect beauty. Those of you who knew Paul are well acquainted with the piercing, penetrating light of his gaze. That light enveloped him ... *became* him.

I trust that Paul was seldom if ever outside the presence of the living Christ—but what happened during those last seven or eight hours in his cell can only be called miraculous. He and I were not alone there; we were bathed in divinity. Without the assistance of the angels, these 62,000 words could never have been uttered, let alone dictated and recorded. And yet, they were, flawlessly.

IX

SAUL

Tarsus, Cilicia

My apprenticeship in my father's business was arduous, but I loved those years. From the age of seven to twelve, I labored just like one of his workers, but harder than any of them—I made sure. In the beginning, I was resentful and bitter, a study in self-pity. My mind played and replayed that humiliation in the synagogue. But, as time passed—with the help of Pylenor, the rhythm of the labor, an elderly goatherder, and the animals themselves—I was healed.

The first two years of my apprenticeship were focused on learning about goats, the mainstay of our business. In spite of my best efforts to dislike these creatures, their vitality, playfulness, and intelligence won me over, and soon I had given them secret names; secret because I knew that they were not pets. In just a few months, two of the finest in the herd would be sacrificed for Yom Kippur, one as a sin offering at the altar, the other driven into the desert. I called these two Moses and Aaron. Only Eli ever heard me call them by name, and he just laughed as they came running.

A Numidian servant, Eli was in charge of the diverse group of more than fifty goatherders Father employed to take care of his thousands of animals. About a year before I was born, Eli had become deathly ill in Egypt. In the strange ways of Providence, it was that illness—and my later discovery of a diagram from that trip—that would catapult my father into the business of making the most sought-after tents in the region. But more on that in a moment.

Although a man of sixty when I began working with him, Eli was extremely agile, and his speed exceeded that of any of the far younger men, especially when chasing a lost kid. A kind, extremely patient man, Eli taught me to recognize the thicker horns of the males and the curl of the lips and change in the urination patterns of the bucks that signaled the beginning of the rutting season. The gentle, intelligent, and social animals quickly came to recognize my voice and come running when I appeared. I was small for my age and still somewhat wary of strangers, but the goats took no notice of these shortcomings. Those years in the pasture rapidly rebuilt my confidence.

Initially, I functioned as just another pair of hands during the spring, when hundreds of does dropped twins and triplets. I became proficient at recognizing the "all belly" signs of pregnancy, and at corralling the young animals into a pen where we could better watch them during kidding season. But it was not until I observed Eli helping young, pregnant does through difficult births that I gained skill and maturity. Over time, I learned ways to handle the animals that even the older and more experienced herders could not mimic. Eli came to trust me with the difficult births of does after one incident in particular when I happened to notice that one of our does was in trouble.

Under normal circumstances, the animals were able to birth their tiny babies without aid from us; their labor and delivery lasted twelve hours or less. But there were times when quick action on our part was required to save both mother and kid. Late one afternoon, I had mounted Karisma and was headed home for supper when I noticed a young female I called Esther on the ground and beginning to push.

Reacting to something I could not name, I dismounted, hobbled Karisma, and studied the situation. By that point, I had witnessed enough births to understand, at the appearance of a little hoof, that the kid was in the breech position. Eli had taught me that under such a circumstance, I should pull very gently with each contraction. Within minutes, I was rewarded with an intact baby curled up in a bubble. *Life!*

Esther quickly licked the sac away, and the new baby was soon suckling heartily. I was hungry and intent on getting home for dinner, but something made me hesitate before remounting Karisma. Sure enough, Esther collapsed to the ground a second time, and I could see a nose and hoof peeking out of her birth canal. It looked as if two more kids were competing to come into the world … one pointed toward the ground and the second one away.

To this day, I credit the divine for inspiring me to reach deeply into Esther's birth canal and push back that nose, permitting the descent and delivery of the first of two males, rapidly followed by the second. I sat there watching the new mother with her babies until dusk, astounded by the beauty and miracle of three brand-new lives.

When he arrived the next morning, Eli did not even attempt to suppress his admiration for my actions of the previous night, insisting that my quick thinking had saved the lives of those two male kids and probably their mother as well. The usually subdued older man was clearly delighted with his star pupil; I'll never forget the sheer joy on his face.

When the rabbi's lots fell on those two males for the Yom Kippur sacrifice later that year, my heart broke. It was a test, I knew. Would I be able to offer up my beloved Moses and Aaron, or would I want to keep the very best for myself, as did Cain? Of course, I dared not utter these thoughts aloud and was grateful that no mortal could read them. But I was confident that the Almighty not only heard my thoughts but could read my heart. That silent struggle was the hardest I have ever fought—harder than withstanding any of the tortures of the last thirty years— for I deeply loved those two precious creatures.

Stone-faced, I sat next to my father and Shimon at the front of the synagogue, reciting maxims Pylenor had taught me. I watched as the rabbi walked Moses over to the east end of the temple, took a long, razor-sharp knife, and slit the innocent's throat. Carefully, he collected the gush of blood in a large golden bowl.

Each morning for the previous six months, I had run to see the kids; had marveled as they grew in size and strength. By the time they were two months old, I had taught them to come when I called their names. By August, their *meh-eh-ehs* had become loud enough for Eli to hear and come running as well, only to shake his head in amusement when he saw that it was just the triplets and me, playing.

Eli had warned me about treating the animals as pets, so, aside from naming my favorites, I had kept my feelings in check. But the intelligence, curiosity, and sheer winsomeness of Moses and Aaron had ultimately made them irresistible to me. Those days when they leaped into my arms and then we frolicked in the pasture were among the happiest of my childhood.

As I endured the ritual sacrifice, my lips continually formed the words of Zeno the Stoic: "Mercy often means giving death, not life." I prayed that Father would not see the tears coursing down my face.

X

On my ninth birthday, Shimon took over from Eli as both my trainer in the business and my teacher of the Torah. Since I was nearing manhood, the pace of my studies increased considerably. Two days and three evenings each week, I studied at home with Pylenor.

Although my workdays stretched from dawn to dusk, I looked forward to my lessons in mathematics, rhetoric, and philosophy. Mainly, I relished the Stoics. Pylenor had sparked this interest a few years earlier when he had taught me about King Leonidas and the Spartans' final courageous battle against the conquering Persian army. It was not the military strategy that had captivated me; that was only mildly interesting. What I hungered for was to learn how to contain my fierce emotions and fiery, passionate nature. In that quest, I took to Zeno, Epictetus, and Cleanthes as if meeting the best of friends. Incrementally, I began to look differently at my humiliation in the synagogue, as well as my relationship with my father and with authority in general.

I can see Pylenor now, the tall, elegant, learned scholar, leaning down to confer with his emotionally volatile pupil as he sat cross-legged on the divan, surrounded by scrolls of the Odyssey and several Stoic philosophers. It was the beginning of our evening study session, and I was brooding, as morose as an eight-year-old can be. My mind was crowded with negative thoughts about my relationship with my father. I found myself obsessively playing and replaying what had happened during our evening meal. Confidently I had recited the Shema, trusting that I had assimilated the wisdom of the Stoics and would be impervious to Father's rection. I looked up at my father, expecting to see some sign of approval. But he simply stared at me intensely, and I was sure he was still reflecting on the blunder I'd made in the synagogue the year before.

My father was a true son of Benjamin, very tall and still muscular, although past sixty. His brow sat like a promontory above black, bushy eyebrows that accentuated the darkness of his deep brown eyes. Although I had been ravenous after my long day with the goats, I found myself suddenly without appetite, staring at the food in front of me and wishing I could disappear—or at least run away to some distant land. I could feel the heat of shame in my cheeks, the emotional turmoil in my belly.

"Eat, son," my father commanded. "Pylenor is here for this evening's session, and you need fuel to study." His voice was naturally loud, but even more so at that moment. I jumped at the sound of it, as did my sisters, who lowered their heads. Obediently I picked at the food that I would have preferred to toss away.

As if conjured by Father's words, Pylenor appeared in the courtyard. "Oh, I apologize for interrupting dinner," he offered, ever gracious. "I must be early."

We were all grateful for the interruption. My sisters scurried about, hastily clearing the table, and soon, my tutor and I were alone in the courtyard. As I collected the scrolls we were studying, I furtively observed Pylenor, who was watching me in return as he waited. When, finally, I was seated among the manuscripts, he asked nonchalantly, "Who succeeded Zeno as leader of the Stoa Poikile?"

I was still so absorbed in thoughts of my father that my tutor had to ask the question again. This time, he qualified it. "Saul, who was the most unlikely successor to Zeno—due to his early career as a wrestler and his lack of aristocratic and financial standing in the Aeropagus?"

"Cleanthes," I responded, almost without thinking. "Despite the predictions of his smarter, wealthier competitors, Cleanthes took over the school upon Zeno's death."

After a moment of silence, Pylenor smiled, coaxing a widening smile from me in return as I considered what my teacher had reminded me of. Cleanthes had been ridiculed by all the other students of the Stoa. He was penniless, with a stocky, "un-Greek" physique—a slow learner whose ability to think had perhaps been affected by blows to the head during wrestling. It was his passion for learning philosophy and internalizing its wisdom that had allowed him to defy the odds. Looking up at my tutor, still grinning, I quoted the Stoic philosopher: "'Steel your sensibilities, so that life shall hurt you as little as possible.'"

Pylenor nodded approvingly.

With the wisdom that comes only with age, I understand now that I am indebted to my father for his insistence that I become a fluent speaker, reader, and writer of both Greek and Latin. In the course of my philosophical studies with Pylenor, I came to see that my anger and resentment toward my father was my choice. Although I was still very young, I understood what Epictetus meant when he wrote that neither criticism nor praise is, in itself, bad or good. Each is neutral in value, imposed from without, and therefore, not within our control. I came to see that, while I could not control either the criticism or the praise leveled at me, I *could* curb my own response to it.

That realization felt incredibly liberating to my young self. Once I'd achieved a sense of freedom from the weight of others' opinions, I resolved to accomplish the primary goal of the Stoic: Equanimity in the face of all things, whether good or evil. I would will myself to see all things as morally neutral. Aside, of course, from the Law. Because I had accepted my father's judgment as real, I had believed myself angry with him. Once I internalized the philosophy of moral neutrality, I knew that it was myself I was angry with, not my father.

XI

When I turned eleven, I aspired to take on new responsibilities involving the weaving of goat cloth. Shimon tried to dissuade me from the endeavor because the goat hair was extremely tough and bristly and tended to cut the hands of the workers. But I was insistent, believing that I could make improvements to the methods our workers used and thereby increase production. Although short, I was strong and had large hands. I could easily experiment with the position of the weaving tool on the board and varying lengths of goat hair. I knew that, on average, it took over three days to produce one tent. I felt I could cut that down to just one day by adjusting the measurements on our weaving boards based on an old diagram I'd found.

Our tents were prized throughout the world for their ability to keep their dwellers warm and dry. The Roman soldiers purchased all we could provide, and desert dwellers had learned to value our tents above any other. We were always behind on orders.

Most of our competitors used goat hair solely inside the tent, to fashion partitions for separating parents from children, soldiers from one another. The tents themselves were composed of animal hides such as sheepskin. When Father and Shimon began making tents, it was as a side business; mainly, they made smaller and cheaper items such as garments, purses, and satchels.

Their first tents were not unlike their competitors': constructed of hides rather than the more labor-intensive goat cloth.

Their discovery of the utility of pure goat cloth tents was accidental. Ten years before, before I was born, Shimon had traveled to Egypt looking for ways to grow the business. Eli—the man who would later teach me all he knew about goat herding—was employed in Shimon's caravan. When Eli became seriously ill on the trip, the group was forced to stop at an oasis in the desert for several days while he recovered. It was there that Shimon met and befriended a Bedouin goatherder who shared the great benefits of tents made of goat hair cilicium. Far more porous than animal hide, the goat hair cloth permitted the circulation of air when the weather was fair, he explained, but when the monsoons came, the tiny openings in the fabric sealed tight and prevented any moisture from coming in.

When Father provided the Tribune with enough of our first goat hair tents for an entire Roman Legion, our business soared. Within just a few weeks, we were unable to produce the necessary volume.

Resurrecting the sketch that Shimon had brought back from the Bedouin, I decided to adjust the position of the four pegs on the large wooden boards we used for weaving. I calculated that, by spreading the distance between the pins while shortening the ends of the cotton cords on the weaving stick, I could speed up the process of making the cloth. When it came time to try out the new method, both Shimon and my father again tried to dissuade me from participating in the new process; they wanted the older, more experienced men to do the experiment.

"You are too young," Shimon insisted. "You will scar your hands."

"Please, Saul," said Father, "a little more money is not worth your health."

But I remained resolute. I knew that none of those men would possess the fortitude to do this. It took me more than five weeks—and almost continual bloody hands—to perfect the system. I adjusted the pegs some forty different times before finding the perfect orientation, but when I finally did, I stunned my uncle and father by making a tent in one day.

At Uncle Shimon's command, all the workers followed my template, and the results were just as I'd hoped. Within three months, we'd caught up on our orders and tripled our profits.

The night that Shimon finished calculating that quarter's profit and expenses happened to be the sabbath. Mother had invited him and his family to dinner after synagogue, and he insisted on making a toast in my honor: "To Saul, our newest partner!"

Because this was a celebratory dinner, Mother and my sisters sat at the long table with the men. Somehow I ended up sitting next to Shimon's daughter, Hannah. "Congratulations, Saul of Tarsus," she whispered.

I turned sharply at the sound of her voice and stared at Hannah. I had not really looked at her in years and was astonished by her womanly beauty. *Hannah,* I thought, *how and when did you stop looking like a bit of girl and begin looking like a—?*

A hush fell over the table, and I sensed my father's eyes on me. I turned to find him smiling. *At me?*

"Son, if you can tear your eyes away from Hannah for a moment, please join us in a toast to your skills—and let us eat!"

XII

Mother's sadness had been building up for weeks. Although her attempt to be joyous at the sabbath dinner of my twelfth birthday had been nothing short of herculean, she wore her melancholy like a shroud. Esther learned quickly that joking about my imminent departure earned her only bitterness.

"Mother!" Esther called out as she cleared the long dinner table of the vestiges of lamb, beef, various cheeses, and a wide assortment of fruits.

"Yes, dear," replied Mother, turning toward her oldest child, the shadow of a smile playing at her lips.

Esther winked at me, her face radiant as she gaily said, "Just think! After tomorrow, we will not have to worry about meals for our picky little Saul!"

Within seconds, Mother was at her side. The slap across Esther's face resounded throughout the courtyard, silencing even the birds. "Wait until you have a child … a son!" she growled. "Your only son!"

Esther stood paralyzed, her hand against the darkening red handprint on her cheek, her eyes welling over. She stared at our mother as if she had transmogrified into a monster.

Mother's eyes were wild. "Don't you ever criticize your brother! Ever!"

My father finally awoke from his stupefaction, and

hastily inserted himself between his wife and daughter. He took Mother by the hand, murmuring softly to her as he led her out of the room.

"Saul!!" cried Esther, her voice quavering with emotion and shock, "I was joking! Just trying to make our mother smile!"

Mother had never before laid a hand on any of us. I could feel tears stinging my own eyes as I opened my arms to gather Esther in.

At dawn, we heard the approach of what sounded like an army—and indeed, this century of Roman soldiers, servants, and pack animals was an army of sorts. Although I knew that Tacitus, the Roman governor of Tarsus, had insisted on sending soldiers to protect us on our journey to Jerusalem, my jaw dropped at the sight of them, magnificent in the early morning light: fifty-odd men on horseback in gleaming scarlet legionnaire uniforms complete with body armor, daggers, swords, javelins, and shields. In the center of the *Equites Legionis* was the carriage where Father and I would be seated for the next thirty to forty days.

More excited than I had ever been, I had slept but an hour or two, continually awakened by the thoughts racing through my head. *Jerusalem! Six years of study at the feet of Gamaliel! Was there a boy in all of Cilicia as fortunate as I?*

I tried and failed to tamp down my fervor. As soon as I heard the voices of my father and one of the soldiers, I grabbed my three bags and raced out to the courtyard, hoping to be gone before Mother awoke. This was a vain hope since I knew that the sound of the troops would have awakened Ezekiel.

Mother's cries soon echoed throughout the still morning air: "I will never see my son again! Please do not take him away! Not yet! He is still just a boy!"

I slowed momentarily, wondering if I should return to the house and embrace her one last time, but Father was already standing in front of the carriage. Correctly interpreting my hesitation, he shook his head.

Although we didn't speak of it, both Father and I feared the toll that extreme grief would take on Mother's health. I knew that her pregnancy with me, while joyous, had been damaging to her forty-five-year-old body. More and more frequently, she needed to rest in the middle of the day. Was she right that we would never see each other again? She'd sounded so sure of it.

After her shocking outburst at Esther the previous night, her shortness of breath had returned, and her lips had turned a disturbing dusky color. Looking back, I would like to think that, had I known her fate, I would have forgone the offer to go off and study at the Temple. But if I am honest, I must admit: even if I had known that my mother would die before my fourteenth birthday, I would still have gone.

There was a pall over us that first seemingly endless day of our journey, and we shared only cursory conversation. I think Father and I feared that speaking about Mother and her terrible lament that morning might bring about what we feared. If we closed our eyes to what was apparent, then perhaps we could keep the worst from happening.

Jostling about on the hard wooden bench of the carriage hour after hour was a lesson in endurance for both Father and me. Accustomed to twelve-hour days of working with the goat-cloth or riding off on Karisma to check our herds, I found sitting in a confined space difficult. After close to fourteen hours of it, I was eager to move about. As soon as we stopped, I sprang out of the coach and down the stairs in the hope that I could get a closer look at the horses ... maybe even help with the work of cooling them down, untacking them, combing them, and picking their hooves.

The soldiers' stallions were majestic and exceedingly well trained. Although their flanks still heaved, they stood patiently waiting after the majority of their riders had dismounted and headed for the tavern and wine. I walked quickly over to the legionnaire who was instructing four man-servants—or maybe they were slaves—in how to care for the animals.

"I have ridden since I was small," I said. "May I be of any help?"

Eyes widening at my use of Latin, the tall soldier smiled and said, "Why not? There is no such thing as too many hands when it comes to getting these creatures combed, watered, and fed. But I think we had better get your father's—"

"Justus, Saul is right," interjected my father, whom I had not heard approach. "He knows horses. In fact, the boy rides better than any of my men and possesses unique skills in relating to animals. His mother and I have often quipped that he prefers them to people!"

Surprised and pleased by his compliments—and his rare use of humor—I glanced over at him, my cheeks burning hot. Noting that his eyes were moist and red-rimmed, I quickly turned my attention back to Justus. *Was Father that worried about Mother? Remorseful for taking me away? Or ... was it possible that his sadness arose from the prospect of not seeing me for six years?*

"All right then, Saul, come on! We have work to do," Justus commanded, stripping off his breastplate, cloak, and weaponry, and handing them to a servant who hovered close behind him. Following his lead, I took off my own outer garments. The temperature had not dropped significantly, and it was very humid.

I strode quickly in the direction Justus indicated, toward the small group of men walking among the herd of at least fifty majestic black stallions, their backs soaked with sweat. We then headed for a large barn about twenty meters from the tavern, and, for the next hour, I busily tended to the animals, my mind emptied of everything but the needs of these fine horses.

At one point, Justus appeared at my shoulder. "Saul," he said, startling me out of my reverie, "your father asked that I come and drag you away from the animals—" He cut himself off when he saw that I was crouched beside the lame Friesian he had told me to avoid. "What in the name of Mars are you doing, Saul? And how is it that this horse hasn't kicked you to the other end of the barn?" His frown was so pronounced that his dark brown eyebrows almost met, and one side of his mouth pulled up into a grimace. "Saul, had I known you would ignore my instruction and work with this injured horse, I would never have ...."

In an instant, I stood and moved out of the creature's way, then whistled to him. The horse came prancing forward, shook his mane, then held up his beautiful tail as if he were in a show.

Justus shook his head in amazement and said, grudgingly, "I see that he is no longer lame, thanks to your ministrations. But as a general rule, we cannot take the time to pick the horses' hooves this way, Saul. It takes far too long."

Without a word, I held up the pick I had fashioned from scrap metal on the farm years earlier. "What if I were to show your servants how to do it quickly?" I asked. "If they follow my directions, it should take no more than an additional five minutes. We can make each of them one of these, to carry in their tunics as I do." I showed him the folds of material that I had fashioned into a protective sleeve of sorts.

Just then, I heard a low chuckle and male voices. I looked in the direction of the sound and saw my father and the centurion picking their way through the piles of hay and other less appealing horse detritus toward us. Hoping he was not annoyed that I hadn't yet come to dinner, I opened my mouth to apologize, but before I could utter a word, Justus said to the centurion, "Maximillian, Saul has been showing me a way to tend efficiently to our lame horses."

Father smiled broadly and put his hand on my shoulder.

He looks proud, I thought. *Proud of me!*

Once smiles and congratulatory comments had been exchanged, Justus offered to let me exercise the stallions that had gotten edgy because they were not being ridden frequently enough. I looked toward Father for approval and saw him nod, still smiling happily, as he launched into the story of my saving the lives of the doe goat and her twin kids. Maximillian stood listening politely.

The only way he could have known about that dangerous birth was from Eli, I thought. *That night at the synagogue ... he must have known that the sacrificial kids were the ones I had saved.*

How much more do you know about me, Father?

The month-long journey seemed considerably shorter because I spent much of it on horseback. Each evening, I worked with Justus's servants as they learned to tend the hooves of the horses with their new picks. Within a week, every one of them was as nimble at the task as I was.

XIII

Jerusalem

Maximillian stopped our caravan so we could rest after the arduous ascent through the pass of Beth-Horons to the Garden of Olives. I had looked out of the opening of the carriage just once as we traversed that road. The gorges on either side were so deep that I saw only a dizzying black abyss.

Although I had studied the Judean War of a few decades earlier, the sight of the place where the Judean army had routed a Roman legion of more than 8,000 men evoked chaotic and paradoxical emotions. Horror, pride, sorrow, and awe competed as I pondered what the battle must have been like: the screams of terrified men and horses, the hundreds of bodies toppling into the bottomless gorges on either side. But, primary among my feelings was pride. Judean warriors had masterfully ambushed the Romans, attacking them with arrows directed with fearsome accuracy. If I—a twelve-year-old boy—was thinking about this battle as we rode, what thoughts must be in the minds of these legionnaires?

The bloody images I'd conjured up were forgotten as I climbed down the stairs of the carriage after Father, into a profound silence. I had become accustomed to the sometimes coarse and always raucous banter of the legionnaires, but today none made a sound. As one, they gazed toward the city below.

Like them, my father and I were speechless at the sight … dumbfounded. Tears coursed down my father's weathered face as we looked down upon her: Zion. The City of David. Jerusalem! This time, I understood that they were tears of gladness. If Father still worried about Mother, I knew he had conquered any regrets over his decision. This journey had been ordained since my birth and was a privilege that neither my father nor his, nor his father before him, had been granted. Mother understood this as well, even if she was moved to protest the inevitable. My concern for my mother had not lessened, even as the anticipation of my new life had grown. I feared that her cries upon our departure had been less a complaint than a portent. What if she were right that we would never see each other again? On top of that, I couldn't help feeling disloyal to Mother when the images I saw in my dreams were not of her … but of Hannah.

"Jerusalem truly is a city befitting the gods," the centurion said softly, breaking the silence.

Even the rowdiest of the soldiers stood transfixed at the splendor of the Temple, which soared into the heavens from the middle of a gigantic pure white stone platform. Its shining dome caught the rays of the setting sun and bathed the blinding white building in an effusion of gold. Rising upward to the west lay Zion's Upper City—King David's home for eternity. I felt my heart would burst for joy. In just one week, it would be Passover, and Father and I would be *here* to celebrate it. Only Father heard as I whispered the words of Jeremiah:

Hear the word of the Lord, O nations,
Proclaim it on distant coasts and say;
He who scattered Israel now gathers them together,
he guards them as a shepherd his flock.
The Lord shall ransom Jacob,
He shall redeem him from the hand of his conqueror.

Shouting, they shall mount the heights of Zion,
They shall come streaming to the Lord's blessings:
the grain, the wine, and the oil,
the sheep and the oxen;
they themselves shall be like watered gardens,
I will lavish choice portions upon the priests,
And my people shall be filled with my blessings,
says the Lord.

Taking the southern route toward the Temple, we descended toward the walled city and entered through one of its massive gateways. I could hear Maximillian exchange greetings with a publican who seemed pleasantly surprised to see fellow Romans arriving.

The last month had been the happiest of days for our coterie of soldiers. The horses were healthier than they had ever been; none was lame, and that was a first. The legionnaires attributed this good fortune to one person: Saul of Tarsus. By the time we reached our destination, they had come to treat me not as a child but as an equal. I believed the rigors and experiences of the journey—and the surprising praise from my father—had prepared me for the intense study that would begin in under a month.

I thought back to Pylenor, our classes, and his intimations that much of the criticism I'd felt coming from my father had existed only in my mind. Perhaps he'd been right. My father was laconic; because he rarely spoke about anything with me, I had habitually inferred his thoughts and opinions from his facial expressions, which were almost always impassive. As I considered him now, I realized that he had trained himself to reveal no emotion. Undoubtedly, this came in handy in doing business— a Jew among the Gentiles—but perhaps it was not as effective in relating to his wife and children.

XIV

I was alternately Rabban Gamaliel's most esteemed student and his most frustrating. During my first two years of study, I was one of a thousand young Jewish boys from families who could afford the hefty costs of Jerusalem Temple training, anonymous, dealing only with the underlings of the Elders of the Sanhedrin. We were divided into two groups: five hundred studying the Torah, five hundred Greek wisdom. Those who made it through their first group could then begin the second. I had chosen to be in the Torah group first because I hoped to persuade my teachers I was already schooled in Greek philosophy, thanks to my years of study with one of the leading Greek tutors. But through either error or providence, I was assigned the group studying Greek philosophy. It would take me two years to move on to Torah study—twenty-four months of mostly wasted time, studying with teachers who were far less schooled than I. By then, I had earned a reputation—one that Father would not approve of. I could not keep silent when the teachers erred when discussing Plato and Zeno. Too many times, I had interrupted a discourse with corrections, thus making myself some enemies.

"How many laws have we about prophecy?"

From my usual spot in the front row, I sprang to my feet and replied, "Fifty-six, Rabban Gamaliel. The prophecy section begins with number 309: 'To heed the call of every prophet in each generation, provided that he neither adds to nor takes away from the Torah, Deuteronomy 18:15. Number 310 is 'Not to prophesy falsely,' Deuteronomy 18:20. Number 311 is 'Not to refrain from putting a false prophet to death nor to be in fear of him, Deuteronomy 18:22. The remaining forty-six laws of the Prophecy section are all negative since they are all prohibitive, beginning with 312: 'Not to make a graven image; neither to make it oneself nor to have it made by others,' Exodus. 20:4—"

"Saul, stop, please," interrupted the Rabban. His exasperation was evident in his expression and the slope of his shoulders. He understood that if he had not intervened, I would have recited the entire section of the Prophecy. "Sit down, Saul," he said with a sigh.

I obeyed, continuing to regard my teacher as he made his best effort to ignore me. I followed the direction of his piercing gaze, up and over my head and about three rows back. *This will not go well,* I thought.

"Stephen, please recite King David's psalm of mercy."

I knew Stephen well enough to wager that he could sit there, scratching his head from that moment until the end of time and would never come up with even one sentence of the psalm. It was the middle of summer, and we were sitting outside in Israel's Court. Stephen was sweating, and so were we all.

Rabban Gamaliel, on the other hand, looked as if he could stand in the blistering sun endlessly.

Faking a paroxysm of coughing, I doubled over, grabbed a stylus and extra wax from under my tunic, and rose, still coughing furiously as I hurried over to the well for a cup of water.

The ruse worked; Gamaliel's penetrating gaze remained on Stephen while I grabbed a stylus and scroll from my tunic inner sleeve and scribbled quickly. Patiently, he prompted, "Stephen, it is number thirty-two. It begins with these two stanzas:

Blessed is the one
whose transgressions are forgiven,
whose sins are covered.
Blessed is the one
whose sin the Lord does not count against them
and in whose spirit is no deceit.

Rabban always closed his eyes when he recited scripture or one of the Prophets, so he did not see me pass by Stephen on my way back to my seat.

Stephen stood up, glanced down, and smiled. "Thank you, Rabban Gamaliel. Yes, I do recall the remainder of King David's hymn to the Lord of Mercy.

When I kept silent,
my bones wasted away
through my groaning all day long.
For day and night
your hand was heavy on me;
my strength was sapped
as in the heat of summer.
Then I acknowledged my sin to you
and did not cover up my iniquity.
I said, "I will confess
my transgressions to the Lord."
And you forgave
the guilt of my sin.
Therefore let all the faithful pray to you
while you may be found ….

As a beaming Stephen took his seat, Rabban Gamaliel looked back at me, then up at Stephen. He frowned but said nothing.

As we began our simple midday meal, I noticed Rabbis

Aaron, Boaz, and Zevulon hurry over to Rabban Gamaliel but thought nothing of it. When we were done, we once again assembled for class.

"For the remainder of the afternoon," said Rabban Gamaliel, "all please study the Nevi'im, specifically, the Book of Job." Then, pointing to a fellow about my age but taller and far quieter, he continued, "Simeon ... in two days, I would like you, Saul, and Stephen, to lead a discussion on Job. You will talk about who Job is meant to represent, why the Lord would make such an agreement with Satan, and list the applications of the story to the nation of Israel today and to us individually." Then he turned to me and said, "Saul, please come with us."

XV

We formed an awkward line in front of a long wooden table covered with scrolls: first came Rabban Gamaliel, then rabbis Aaron, Boaz, and Zevulon, then me. Rabban pointed over to a couch, indicating that I should sit, while the three far younger rabbis—my early Greek philosophy teachers—remained standing beside him, looking tense.

Taking the proffered seat, I glanced around the apartment that Gamaliel and Caiaphas shared, thinking about the challenge of sharing living space with someone whose beliefs are dissimilar—in this case, radically so.

Caiaphas only rarely appeared in front of our classes, and when he did, he lectured on the Torah: Genesis, Exodus, Leviticus, Numbers, or Deuteronomy. As I reflected on the living arrangement of the two men, I was struck by Gamaliel's shrewdness and practicality in selecting a dominant roommate with vastly different interpretations of the faith. To us young Hebrew boys, the theological differences between the Sadducee and Hillel Pharisee were irrelevant to our foundation in the Torah. Nor did we need to appreciate the political ambitions of Caiaphas and his Sadducee followers, or their opposition to Gamaliel's favored method of study. But to serious scholars in the Temple, passionate debate on these matters was food and drink. In choosing to share his priestly quarters with Caiaphas, Gamaliel personified the wisdom of keeping his enemy closer than his friend.

As often happened when I was anxious, my attention was scattered, and I found myself thinking about home, my mother, the farm, the goats—and wondering how everything was going in my absence ....

My ruminations were cut short when I heard Rabbi Aaron say, "Saul?" Clearly, he had been speaking to me, but I had not listened to a word he'd said. In fact, my thoughts had turned to the letter I'd written Hannah the night before. Had I chosen my words wisely? Written appropriately?

Hannah had written to me each week since I'd arrived— a total of 156 letters. I had answered only two. Her first and last. At fifteen, like most of the other students in the Temple, I found I had to pay the utmost attention to my studies. And yet ... the changes overtaking my body were potent, at times overwhelming. Hannah was just two years younger than I, and her letters could stimulate my imagination as nothing ever had. Not that any of her words were less than chaste. Perhaps it was the very guile-lessness of them that captivated me, as she wrote lightly and cheerily of her life, studies, family, and the goats.

"Saul!" the rabbi barked once more.

I jumped at the command and sprang up.

The four men stood in a line glaring at me, and the silence stretched on. The expressions on the two youngest men grew fierce. It was evident that they expected me to say something, but, as I had no idea of what I was doing in front of my interrogators, I stood straight and tried to get my mind off of Hannah and onto what could possibly be the problem. Then it came to me: *One of the three must have seen me copy and then give the psalm to Stephen.*

But, if this were the case, the anger displayed on their faces seemed out of proportion. Hadn't I just helped out a fellow student in need? Surely, they understood that Stephen, especially, might benefit from some prompting, having not had the benefit of the kind of home-schooling most of us had enjoyed.

At a loss, I continued to hold my tongue as the minutes stretched on. Rabbis Boaz and Zevulon finally turned away from me and toward Rabban Gamaliel, heaving dramatic sighs. They both extended their arms in a gesture of sheer frustration at having to deal with me.

Finally, Rabban Gamaliel spoke. "Saul, this is not our first conversation about your performance in our classes, is it?"

"No, Rabban."

"Do you recall our first?"

"Of course, I do!" *How could I possibly have forgotten such a thing?*

"Tell me about it, Saul."

"You do not remember, Rabban?" I asked him, puzzled.

He shook his head, trying not to smile, and said, "Saul … I do remember. I merely want to hear you tell it."

"You told me that I was fortunate to have had the depth of tutoring I'd had before coming to the Temple, and reminded me that many others had not enjoyed such a privilege. You also praised my gift of memory, which exceeded that of any of your other students. You told me that I should keep these facts in mind when answering questions and during class discussions." My mind raced back to our class earlier that day, and I understood that I had not followed this admonition. "Rabban, I apologize for my thoughtlessness when you asked about the Prophecy section. I see now that I may have been flaunting my gifts in front of my fellow students, as you advised me not to do. That will not happen again."

Gamaliel's smile at my apology warmed me, but I could see that the younger men were still not satisfied. They shook their heads vigorously, causing their long beards to sway side to side.

Unable to contain himself any longer, Rabbi Zevulon cried out, "Saul, do you admit that you cheated today?"

Bewildered, I looked at the man, who could not be more than five or six years older than I. Certainly, he was younger than twenty-one. "Cheated? What do you mean, *cheated*?"

A torrent of words exploded out of his mouth, most of which I could not make out through his rage. Spittle flew, and he sputtered, "Do you deny … Psalm Thirty-two … Stephen …

.

"Rabbi Zevulon," I interjected, hoping to stem the tide of his rage, "I beg your pardon for making you so obviously angry." This was somewhat disingenuous, as I'd understood immediately that it was not my actions that had inspired this torrent of invective; it was his jealousy of his fifteen-year-old student. Zevulon was no scholar; his lack of understanding of the Greek philosophers was startling. Because of his intellectual limitation, he was defensive and easily threatened, and this, in my opinion, made him a terrible teacher. I believed he lacked the ambition and discipline to become another Gamaliel. If I could have gotten away with it, I would have laughed. Instead, I said calmly, "Yes, Rabbi. When I saw that Stephen was incapable of answering Rabban's question, I helped him. I do not believe that helping is cheating."

By this point, my nemesis had exhausted himself. Quietly, Rabban Gamaliel stepped in, asking, "Saul, why did you do this? Why did you attempt to deceive us?"

Looking fixedly at Rabban Gamaliel, then at Aaron and the others, I asked, "Did I not fulfill two of our Laws with my actions? Does number thirty-three not command that we not put any Jew to shame? And number thirty-five prohibits us from allowing the simple-minded to stumble on the road—is that not correct?"

XVI

Stephen and I eyed each other as we followed Simeon out of the Temple, across the bridge to the Upper City, and through Ginnoth Gate. Clearly, he was heading for the Upper City on Mount Zion. Simeon had approached Stephen and me immediately upon cessation of classes for the day and suggested that we go to his home to prepare our assignment on the Book of Job.

We knew practically nothing about one another, aside from the bare facts: Stephen was four years older than Simeon and I, and was from Galilee; I was from Tarsus, and Simeon lived in Jerusalem. The work expected of each student hindered all but the most casual of conversations.

After fifteen minutes or so, we passed by the Upper Market, then followed Simeon down a long, narrow, winding road. Finally, we stopped in front of an imposing, white-walled house.

Shifting from one foot to the other, tall, gangly Simeon looked everywhere but at Stephen or me. "Let me guess," Stephen said, laughing, "you forgot to tell us that your grandfather is Annas and your father, the High Priest Caiaphas."

Dark brown eyes huge, Simeon gulped and said, "No, no ...not Caiaphas. My ... father ... is Rabban Gamaliel."

"Your *father is Rabban Gamaliel?*" Stephen and I both squeaked out simultaneously. "And this is *his* house we are going to study in?" Stephen nodded toward the door, staring at it balefully.

"Stephen, let's go do this," I said, trying to sound nonchalant. "The Book of Job is not one of my favorites ... but ... Rabban assigned it to the three of us, so what are we to do? Simeon probably told him we would be coming here to prepare ..." I looked over at Simeon, willing him to nod his agreement, but got only a stare in return. "We have a lot of work to do, and we have maybe four hours of light left."

Simeon opened the door, and the three of us filed into the courtyard. As we headed toward the house, Stephen and I took in the beautiful flowers and trees, and the three impressive staircases leading to various parts of the vast edifice.

"Simeon, what a lovely place!" I exclaimed, noting to myself that the surroundings bore the distinct imprint of a woman—his mother, no doubt. She clearly had elegant taste, just as my own mother did. For a moment, I could not breathe, and the tears I had never shed upon her death built up like a colossal dam clogging my throat. I leaned over and coughed, hoping to dislodge the blockage, which only served to bring on an unstoppable paroxysm of deep, hacking coughs.

For the first time in over two years, I heard my mother's cries:

"I will never see my son again!"

"Please do not take him away!"

"Not yet!"

"He is still just a boy!"

I was unable to stem the tide of tears gushing down my face. Through my pain, I heard someone call, "Mother!" and noted that it must be Simeon. Just as I was about to lose consciousness, I felt a hard blow that knocked me to the ground, then another to my back. I lay on my side, eyes closed as my breathing returned to normal, trying to ignore the ferocious pain in my back and chest.

"Saul, open your eyes and look at me."

I did as I was commanded. Blinking frantically to clear my blurred vision, I extended my right hand and struggled to get to my knees.

"Don't get up, not just yet," said the same female voice. "Take a few deep breaths first." She began to count, and I synchronized my breathing to the rhythm of her words. Slowly, the pain receded, my vision cleared, and I could breathe. I blinked rapidly at the woman standing before me. I had been choking and was losing consciousness. She had seen what was happening and calmly taken rapid, effective action ... unlike my mother, who would have been paralyzed, maybe even hysterical.

She smiled. "Hello, Saul. Nice to meet you. Simeon has been talking about you for many months. I am Sarah, Gamaliel's wife, and Simeon's mother." Continuing to speak as serenely as if we sat around a dinner table, she continued, "Now ... can you sit up?"

As I did so, I saw Simeon and Stephen standing a few feet away, by a group of olive trees, regarding me with relief. Suddenly feeling ludicrous, I began to apologize profusely. "I am so sorry for causing a scene ... I don't know what overtook me ...."

Waving my words away, Simeon's mother turned toward a marble table behind her, lifted the steaming carafe that sat there, and poured something into a cup. "Saul, this is very hot, but it will soothe your throat and chest. Just take small sips." She smiled again at me, then at her son and Stephen. "Now, where are you boys planning to study?" Pointing at a long wooden table, she said, "How about here? This will leave me room to bring out your dinner in a few minutes."

"Yes, thank you, Mother," said Simeon. "That will work well, I think." Reaching into his pouch, he retrieved a large scroll and placed it at one end of the table. "Here is our friend, Job. Stephen, why don't you read the first chapter out loud?"

Those two young men became my best friends that day. I knew they could not have missed my tears; both probably understood that there had been something more than a particle lodged in my throat. But neither they nor Sarah pressed me about it. My gratitude for this was more than could be spoken.

XVII

"We are told from the start that Job is blameless and upright. He fears God and eschews evil. Consequently, Job has been blessed by God with seven sons and three daughters. Wealthier than any man in the east, Job owns 7,000 sheep, 3,000 camels, and 500 donkeys.

"On feast days, upon rising early in the morning, Job makes burnt offerings, one for each of his children, fearing that they may have sinned and blasphemed God in their thoughts.

"Upon his return from roaming the earth, the Lord initiates a conversation with the Adversary, asking him if he has noticed His servant Job. Going on to extoll him, God declares that there is no one like Job on earth: blameless and upright, fearing God and avoiding sin.

"'But,' challenges the Adversary, 'why would not Job fear you? You have fenced him in with your blessings so that all in his household prosper, and his possessions stretch over the land. Lay your hand on him and see how quickly he blasphemes you.'

"You will recall that disaster then strikes. God accepts Satan's challenge to test Job: Is Job's reverence for God contingent on his manifold blessings? To determine this, the Lord permits Satan to rain down all kinds of calamity on Job; he strikes his children, his livestock, all that Job holds dear. The man is subjected to all manner of physical suffering—but still he does not blaspheme."

Rabbi Zevulon paused and smiled at the group of sixty young scholars before him. "Rabban Gamaliel assigned Stephen, Simeon, and Saul to lead a discussion on the oldest book of the Torah," he explained, "the book of Job. They, in turn, asked that I set the scene with a brief narration of the Prologue—a passage that we all know well, but that bears repeating." The rabbi paused again, waiting for the predictable shifting in seats, downcast eyes, nervous coughs.

"Gentlemen, this will not be a directed discussion, as is our usual method of study. Instead, your three colleagues have prepared a play of sorts, so that you might observe, listen, and learn. They intend to present three points of view in answer to Rabban's assigned questions: *Who is Job meant to represent? Why would the Lord agree to Satan's proposal?* And, *How might we apply the lessons of Job's experience to our own lives and the life of Israel?* At the end of their presentation, you will be asked to decide as a group if these questions have been answered satisfactorily."

Rabbi Zevulon bowed toward Rabban Gamaliel and then toward the assembled group, before turning to the three of us, seated in the front row. He clapped his hands just once and said, "Gentlemen, please begin," then took a seat, smiling at his own performance.

It had been my idea to ask Rabbi Zevulon to participate in our little play. I had given considerable thought to his comment that I had cheated when providing Stephen with the material he should have known as a third-year student. I'd also recalled the fact that, more than once, Rabban had mentioned my "feats of memory" and expressed his concern that they could someday cause me problems, perhaps even grief.

During our long and sleepless night at Simeon's house,

my two friends and I had considered several methods of approaching our assignment. Stephen and Simeon favored a traditional lecture and debate, but as they tried to convince me of this—perhaps because of my earlier episode—I found myself bone-weary and only half-listening to their arguments.

I interrupted Stephen's third attempt to assign one of the points to each of us. "Why not act it out?" I blurted. I spelled out my idea, and here we were.

Taking Rabbi Zevulon's lead, Stephen stood and bowed. "Rabban, you asked that we explain what Job represents. We believe that Job is an archetype. As such, he represents each man who lives ... has ever lived ... and will live until the end of time." Although he held the scroll on which his speech was written, he spoke with flair, seemingly extemporaneously.

Now, when it mattered, Stephen sounded like a professional actor who proclaimed such speeches daily. He spoke slowly and effectively, made use of pauses and gestures. To be sure, Stephen relied on the scroll, but—perhaps in part because of his strong Galilean accent—his commentary on the universality of Job and the disagreements among scholars about his existence came across as charming. Within minutes, the fact that he consulted a written text faded into the background, and he held his audience rapt. I was almost disappointed when, with a flourish, he concluded his remarks and introduced Simeon and me.

Both of us stood, turned our backs, and stripped off our robes. Underneath, Simeon was in sackcloth and ashes and had painted on himself bright red sores that looked quite realistic from a distance. I was dressed in an ordinary tunic and cloak.

Simeon collapsed on the tile floor, head in his hands, and cried out:

Know now that God hath overthrown me, and hath 'com-

passed me with his net. Behold, I cry out of wrong, but I am not heard: I cry aloud, but there is no judgment. He hath fenced up my way that I cannot pass, and he hath set darkness in my paths. He hath stripped me of my glory, and taken the crown from my head. He hath destroyed me on every side, and I am gone, and mine hope hath he removed like a tree. He hath also kindled his wrath against me, and he counteth me unto him as one of his enemies. His troops come together, and raise up their way against me, and encamp round about my tabernacle. He hath put my brethren far from me, and mine acquaintances are verily estranged from me. My kinsfolk have failed, and my familiar friends have for-gotten me. They that dwell in mine house, and my maids, count me for a stranger: I am an alien in their sight. I called my servant, and he gave me no answer; I entreated him with my mouth. My breath is strange to my wife, though I entreated for the children's sake of mine own body. Yea, young children despised me; I arose, and they spake against me. All my inward friends abhorred me: and they whom I loved are turned against me. My bone cleaveth to my skin and to my flesh, and I am escaped with the skin of my teeth. Have pity upon me, have pity upon me, O ye my friends; for the hand of God hath touched me. Why do ye persecute me as God, and are not satisfied with my flesh?

Oh that my words were now written! Oh that they were printed in a book! That they were graven with an iron pen and lead in the rock forever! For I know that my redeemer liveth, and that he shall stand at the latter day upon the earth: And though after my skin worms destroy this body, yet in my flesh shall I see God: Whom I shall see for myself, and mine eyes shall behold,

and not another; though my veins be consumed within
me. But ye should say, Why persecute we him, seeing
the root of the matter is found in me? Be ye afraid of the
sword: for wrath bringeth the punishments of the sword,
that ye may know there is a judgment.

I reached into my cloak, pulled out a large handful of
dirt, and threw it on Simeon's bowed head. Once the gasps,
inhalations, and murmured exclamations subsided, I stomped
around Simeon's bent body, then lifted my unshod foot and
pushed him with it—just enough to stir up my audience once
again. Next, I lowered the hood of my cloak from my head and
roared, "You see that I look like you! Dress like you! But I am
your Adversary!"

Crouching down, I pretended to whisper something into
Simeon's ear, then jumped straight up as if on springs. "I am the
Lord's Adversary. Ever since my success in the Garden, I delight
in making just men blaspheme; in tricking upright men into
believing that following God's Law is foolhardy and that He
has no concern for them or their wholly unimportant nation of
Israel. Chosen people, indeed! Why do you think the ten tribes
were scattered? Why do you think Judah's men refused to listen
to him and left for Egypt, only to be SOLD INTO SLAVERY?!"

My classmates seemed either riveted or horrified—perhaps both. I did not dare a glance at Rabban Gamaliel.

Simeon and I then alternated recitations from Job and a
variety of prophets who had predicted the doom of our beloved
nation. Finally, I shouted, "My joy is in defeating your trust in
your Lord, MY ENEMY. Job has lost everything, thanks to me!
And he WILL walk away from this Lord who permitted him to
suffer so. Watch!"

I nodded to Simeon, who stood up and removed his
sackcloth to reveal yet another tunic, this one pure white. He

stood straight and extended his arms as if to embrace all who listened. His expression wholly beatific, he practically sang:

I know that thou canst do everything and that no thought can be withholden from thee. Who is he that hideth counsel without knowledge? Therefore have I uttered that I understood not; things too wonderful for me, which I knew not. Hear, I beseech thee, and I will speak: I will demand of thee, and declare thou unto me. I have heard of thee by the hearing of the ear: but now mine eye seeth thee. Wherefore I abhor myself, and repent in dust and ashes.

At his words, I crumpled to the ground in a heap, head buried in my arms.

Stephen returned to the front of the room, unrolled yet another scroll, and read, "Most of us recall Job's words to his wife following his infestation with boils over his entire body: 'Shall we receive good from the Lord and shall we not receive evil?'"

As before, Stephen's measured, Galilean-accented Aramaic was captivating. Peeking at our audience from between my fingers, I could see that even Rabban Gamaliel was rapt.

"Saul, Simeon, and I have acted out the incredible suffering inflicted on Job," he continued. "We have attempted to show the anguish and agony that surely must have seemed as if they would never end—and yet functioned as a revelation. The Job we have walked with is a different man after his battle with the Adversary. He seems to understand the majesty of our Lord as profoundly as King David:

But I am a worm and not a man,
scorned by everyone, despised by the people.
All who see me mock me;
they hurl insults, shaking their heads.

"He trusts in the Lord," they say,
"let the Lord rescue him.
Let him deliver him,
since he delights in him."
From you comes the theme of my praise in the great
assembly;
before those who fear you,I will fulfill my vows.
The poor will eat and be satisfied;
those who seek the Lord will praise him—
may your hearts live forever!
All the ends of the earth
will remember and turn to the Lord,
and all the families of the nations
will bow down before him ....

Stephen had outdone himself; neither Simeon nor I could have imagined the aplomb and elegance with which he would enact his part. I watched as Stephen signaled Rabbi Zevulon, who strode back to the front of the room, positively beaming at the entire assembly. He even paused to lean over me and shine that huge smile!

Then the rabbi made a sweeping gesture with both arms and said:

So the Lord blessed the latter end of Job more than his
beginning: for he had fourteen thousand sheep, and six
thousand camels, and a thousand yoke of oxen, and a
thousand she asses. He also had seven sons and three
daughters. And he called the name of the first, Jemima;
and the name of the second, Kezia; and the name of the
third, Keren-happuch. And in all the land were no women
found so fair as the daughters of Job: and their father
gave them inheritance among their brethren. After this
lived Job a hundred and forty years and saw his sons,

and his sons' sons, even four generations. So Job died, being old and full of days.

Rabbi Zevulon leaned down and pulled me up off the floor so that I stood beside him. Turning to me, he bowed and stretched out both arms, then brought his hands together in a loud clap. Then, turning to Stephen, he bowed and clapped again. Finally, he offered Simeon the same tribute. Soon the entire class was on its feet, applauding and cheering.

XVIII

AURELIUS

Mamertine Prison, Rome

"Aurelius, you were dismayed—enraged, even—when you learned that I have not always been celibate, but once lived as a married man with children! Why would you ask for more details about a life you believed to be unfitting for a man of God?"

"I am sorry, Rabbi. In that judgment, I was wrong. Wholly wrong."

Paul looked at me almost tenderly, his ravaged features suddenly softer. "What makes you think that Christians who I will never meet should know about my life with Hannah and our children?"

At the phrase, *our children,* his breath caught, and he blinked rapidly.

Almost forty years, and I can see that his grief is as raw, as fresh as if it all happened today. I stared at the man who had saved my life and that of many others, a man who would continue, through the ages, to bring those who are lost—and know it—to Christ. I understood now that I had to choose my words carefully. My reaction to the particulars of his personal story had affected him deeply, far more so than I understood at the time.

"In your letter to the Romans, you write about *good*

zeal," I said, smiling inwardly at the widening of his eyes. "I was filled with the opposite of good zeal when I reacted as I did; when I learned you had once lived the life of an 'ordinary man,' enjoying the sensual congress of a woman, the joy of your own children."

I paused for his comment, but he said nothing—simply keep listening.

"This ... I will call it *evil zeal* for lack of a better name, is dangerous, for it commands something other than the ordinary human life of man and woman for holiness. It denies the sacred partnership that they form with the Creator. It propagates a vicious lie—that all men—and women, too—must forego the solace of marriage and family, the creative partnership, to enter the Kingdom of Heaven. Why ... it asks that they live the unthinkable life that you yourself have suffered for the past few decades: a life of torture, starvation, and imprisonment!"

I stared at this man I had come to love, to revere, with tears in my eyes. "I was born a warrior," I continued, "and so yearn to make the noble sacrifice of mind and body—as you have done. In reparation. The notion is seductive—especially for warriors like me—but entirely wrong. This last letter of yours must be a message filled with His truth, which is love. The joy of His creation."

I had one more thing I was compelled to say, though I felt uncomfortable doing so. We stood regarding each other while I considered my choice of words carefully. "Rabbi ... I believe there is another reason why you must tell of your love for Hannah and the children."

"And what might that be?" Paul asked, his eyes narrowing almost imperceptibly.

After a sharp intake of breath, I plunged in. "In your letter to the Corinthians, you indicate that it is better for a man to remain unmarried ... celibate. Specifically, you write, 'I should like you to be free of anxieties. An unmarried man is anxious about the things of the Lord, how he may please the Lord … I am telling you this for your own benefit, not to impose a restraint upon you, but for the sake of propriety and adherence to the Lord without distraction … a married man is anxious about the things of the world, how he may please his wife, and he is divided .…'"

Paul frowned and narrowed his gaze further, studying me as if taking my measure anew. Then he nodded slowly. "Yes, I did write those words," he said quietly.

Although clearly startled by my recitation, Paul seemed to like the fact that I had committed his words to memory. At least, I hoped he did. Paul looked down at the hardscrabble dirt floor of his cell, obviously musing about what I had said. "Aurelius," he answered after what seemed an eternity but was probably just a minute or two, "of course, you speak correctly." There was admiration in his piercing eyes. "This understanding has come not from you but *through* you, from the Spirit. I find myself compelled to tell you—and our eventual readers—about my ten-year-long marriage to Hannah and how it came to be."

I could see the sheen of unshed tears in his eyes. Dropping his voice to the barest whisper so that I had to lean forward to hear him, he said, "It is not good for man to be alone … man and woman were created to be one. By their very nature, women are closer to God than men. They understand what constitutes love … the impossibly paradoxical ingredients of it—He fashioned them for love."

Unable to resist, I enveloped his emaciated body in my arms. "Thank you, Rabbi," I exhaled.

Paul gently disentangled himself and leaned back so he could peer into my eyes. "You must promise me something, Aurelius," he said.

Surprised, I stepped back to regard him. "Yes, what is it?"

"You must promise me that you will marry."

I stared at him dumbfounded, mouth agape. The right side of his mouth twitched as if he were about to smile, but he said nothing, just continued to look at me. Finally, he asked, "Do I need to repeat myself, Aurelius?"

"No Rabbi, of course not. But why do you ask me to make this pledge?"

Eyes dancing, the holy man chuckled. "After all that we have shared this night, do you honestly need my answer to that question?"

Laughing, I shook my head. "No, I guess not! And yes, I promise you that I will marry."

How could I have dreamt I would meet my very own Hannah?

XIX

SAUL

Jerusalem

Clothed in white linen pants, tunic, and hat, with belts woven of scarlet, purple, blue, and fine white linen, Simeon, Stephen, Yuval, Uri, and I stood in the Holy Place offering *zebach sh'lamim.* I could barely breathe as I gazed in awe at the golden back wall of the porch, golden lamp hanging above, and two tables, one gold, and one marble.

Israel had ten new rabbis on this day, and the five of us were chosen to lead the procession into the Hall to offer gratitude to God for his boundless mercy. We had been preparing for this day for a week by, among other things, selecting an unblemished lamb and sacrificing it, making sure to remove all the fat surrounding the organs for a separate offering to God, by the Law of Moses:

> *You shall make an altar of earth for Me, and you shall sacrifice on it your burnt offerings and your peace offerings ….*

Since our sacrifice was a grateful peace offering, all of the meat would be consumed on this day, with our families, who waited outside in the Court of the Israelites and Court of the Women. Rabbis Gamaliel, Aaron, Boaz, Zevulon, and many I did not know followed us into the Hall, then processed ahead of us but stopped short and stood reverently in front of the veil separating us from the Holy of Holies, where the High Priest Caiaphas had performed the actual sacrifice.

Aside from the occasional hiss and crackle of the burning fat, there was no sound in the hall, and the quiet was profound. The prayers of the High Priest were inaudible to us as he divided up the animal into specified sections for the priests and sons of Israel. Standing between Stephen and Simeon, I risked a glance at each of them in turn, but both had their eyes closed in prayer.

It has been six years, I marveled to myself. *In one way, it feels like six lifetimes, and yet I clearly recall my days of running along the beach of the Tarsus coast with my sisters, playing hide-and-seek behind the dunes.*

Looking around at the lambent glow of the golden-walled hall, I felt like an imposter. I wondered if the rows of rabbis in front of me had ever felt the same. *A rabbi?* How was I prepared to lead a synagogue or provide direction to other Jews? It seemed absurd. I was the same man, Saul of Tarsus, now as when I had arrived here at twelve. And yet, I was not. My eighteenth birthday had come and gone just the week before, marking me a mature man.

Stephen and I locked eyes, and I could not hold back my smile. This man, so different from me in looks, background, and nature, had unexpectedly become my best friend—most likely because of my impulsive gesture in the classroom years earlier. Had I not risked my own future by writing down that psalm for him, would we have become such good friends? More to the point, why had I done such a thing? I still did not know the answer. He, too, would marry this week, but unlike me, he would return home to Galilee for the ceremony.

At the sound of the veil opening, my ponderous thoughts scattered, and my mouth watered at the aroma of roasted lamb.

Like everyone else, I had fasted for the previous two days. Each of us looked up and raced forward to assist Caiaphas in bringing out the central portion of the meal to our waiting families.

Rabbi Zevulon waylaid me as I descended the stairs eastward toward the Court of the Israelites. "Saul," he said, "I want you to know how pleased I was to hear the words Rabban Gamaliel said about you at our small classroom gathering before we left to come here." His eyes were squinting from the sun, which shone directly into his eyes. His grip on my arm was surprisingly forceful as he quoted Gamaliel: "… a student of such distinction that I want him to know that Saul of Tarsus is a welcome member of the rabbinate and of the Sanhedrin now and as long as I am a voting member."

We stood awkwardly on the steps holding our cooling meats, but I could see that the Rabbi had more to say. "For the twelve years that I have lived in the Temple," he continued, "first as a student, then as rabbi, I hoped I could be looked upon with the favor that you have earned from Rabban."

Uncomfortable with this unexpected praise from a man I knew had questioned my integrity and moral character, I started to utter some perfunctory reply so I could make my leave, but he leaned in closer. "I want you to know that I agree with him, Saul. Indeed, I did have serious doubts about your moral caliber at first … but now I would consider it a privilege to work by your side should you ever decide to take Rabban's offer and teach here. The Lord has not given you such prodigious gifts only to see you retreat to Tarsus and a life of herding goats. Ah, well … for now, it seems, that is what He has you doing. But the world will hear of Saul of Tarsus one day … of that, I am certain."

As I stood speechless, Zevulon's thin, planed face broke into a smile surrounded by a wreath of wrinkles. "Go, Job scholar," he said, releasing my arm at last. "Hasten to your bride."

XX

Dear Hannah,

I apologize for my delay in answering your letters. You should know that I have read each of them multiple times. You have asked if I was well, concerned that my silence resulted from ill-health or from being overwhelmed by my studies. In truth, these provided me with facile justifications for my cowardice.

Your warmth, openness, and purity of heart reveal themselves to me through your consistent guilelessness. For example, in your letter before last, you wrote that you felt that your destiny was to be wife to me, and mother to our sons. You wrote that you have felt this way since childhood. Hannah—I have read that letter repeatedly. Each time, I am struck anew with the courage and intensity of spirit I have lacked.

So, no, my dear Hannah, my silence has been due neither to poor health nor to the burden of my studies. I confess that I have enjoyed these years of intellectual boyhood, of the freedom of wholly focusing on the Torah, of concerning myself with nothing but my long-held dream of becoming a rabbi here at the Temple. And, like Jeremiah, embracing life-long celibacy as an offering to the Lord.

But ... here is what I must tell you. The last several months have expunged those fantasies. I know now that I do not possess the nature for the exhaustive discussion of the minutiae of scripture required for such a life. I confess that my mind continually wanders during those interminable and monotonous discussions of the permutations of the Law.

More importantly, I can no longer deny the content of my actual dreams. They are filled with visions of your lovely face, and the changes in your body that my mind imagines have taken place over the past six years. And yes, I dream of the consummation of a love I have long denied.

I ask this next in steadfast hope: Will you agree to be my wife and the mother to our children? (May they, in truth, be sons!)

Not long after my bride-to-be received my letter, our betrothal or *erusin* commenced. Since Father and Hannah's father were full business partners, the traditional *mohar*—the payment from the father of the groom to the father of the bride—was dispensed with, as were the customary gifts from groom to bride. Our week-long wedding was scheduled to take place in the Temple some ten months after I proposed, the day I graduated from my studies.

Today.

On my twenty-minute walk from the Court of the Priests to that of the Women's Courts to meet my bride and our two families, I had time to reflect on Rabban Gamaliel's surprising proposal following the formal cessation of class. Rabban had asked that I wait while he changed his robe, then accompany him on the walk to the hall. As I bided my time, I looked around at the room filled with empty chairs. The long tables were laden with Talmudic scrolls, carefully arranged for the next onslaught of young, eager men. Subtle swirls and concentric circles of roses decorated the mosaic floor. A penetrating sense of nostalgia overtook me, and I grew melancholy as I thought about the boy who had arrived here six years earlier.

As if on cue, Rabban Gamaliel threw open the doors of the priests' apartments to declare a most generous offer. "Saul, since you refuse my invitation to join me in teaching at the Temple, then I insist that your wedding be held at my home. I would like to give you and your bride my blessing during the ceremony. And Sarah and I welcome both your family and Hannah's to stay at our home while they are here in the city."

I gazed mutely at Rabban Gamaliel, overwhelmed at the invitation. I had planned that our marriage be celebrated— and consummated—at Father's home in Tarsus, though the journey would take five or six weeks. *Rabbis do not officiate at weddings,* I thought. *And inviting all nine of us to stay seems unthinkable!*

Reading my thoughts, Gamaliel said, "Our home is substantial, Saul. We have room for all of you with room to spare." His gaze lightened, and his eyes shone as he continued. "And … we'd like to invite you and your bride to spend the appointed seven days of seclusion in our private apartment." When he saw that I was overcome, Gamaliel took my hand and held it gently. "Please accept this wedding gift from Sarah, Simeon, and me."

Quite abruptly, I reached my destination. Amid a swarm of pilgrims stood a group of eight tall people, two white-haired and bearded men; the others, gracefully dressed and veiled women. They were Father, my four sisters, Shimon, his wife Leah, and my own wife-to-be, Hannah.

"Hannah," I said tenderly, standing in front of the veiled woman. She was now close to my height, and I could see the graceful outlines of her form underneath the light violet linen robe. I had never felt more gawky or uncouth than I did at that moment, suddenly aware of my too-large nose, jutting brow, and wholly unattractive countenance. *How is it that a beautiful creature like you wants to marry me? Where is the chubby little girl I left behind in Tarsus?*

Flouting the tradition of keeping her face veiled during the week before marriage, Hannah raised both arms and threw back the hood of her pale violet *halug*. Then, she took three steps forward so that our bodies nearly pressed against each other. As I drank in the rich luster of her hair, the impossibly dewy softness of her skin, Hannah tipped her face up to mine and then—most improperly—kissed me squarely on my lips! Her eyes were a molten combination of copper and dark and light browns, and the softness of those lips was like nothing I had ever experienced or even imagined. Before I could react, as if aware of the boundary she had overstepped, she withdrew back again, hands covering her lips like a child caught doing something she should not. Then she dropped her head so that the mass of her black, soft curls created a new veil for her face.

I did not think. I simply reacted to the fire kindled within me. "Oh, no, wife of mine, " I murmured as I took one long stride forward. I pressed that supple, velvety body to my own, tipped her face upward toward mine, and pressed my lips to hers—abandoning myself to an intensity I had never known.

Placing her palms firmly against my chest, she pushed us apart, laughing merrily as she did so. "Saul, I will make you the best wife in all of Cilicia!" she cried, her voice sounding like the peal of bells.

Reeling with desire, I could feel the flames visible on my face as I worked to regain mastery of my body. The heat intensified when, for the first time, I looked over at my father and Hannah's parents. As I opened my mouth to express apologies for such unseemly behavior, Shimon stepped toward me.

"Saul," he said, reaching out to clasp my hand in both of his, "you have always felt like a son to me." My father's business partner seemed untouched by the passage of the years.

His warm gray eyes overflowed with affection. Once again—as at the synagogue on that long-ago day that marked my seventh birthday—he had stepped between me and humiliation. "Now, your marriage will make it so. Congratulations on all you have accomplished in these last six years. We are all so very proud."

I couldn't help feeling that this dear man was in truth a father to me.

Still standing quietly near the stairs leading down to the Women's Courts were my father and Hannah's mother, Leah. The years had weighed heavily on Father, who was stooped and looked a decade older than Shimon, although he was younger. I approached him and said what I should have many years before. "Father, how do I thank you for these years of education, for this precious training you have provided me?"

He did not reply, but I saw his world-weary eyes fill with tears.

"Saul!" The shout was Esther's. She and my sisters rushed forward to greet and congratulate me.

XXI

When our wedding party stepped through the western wall of the Temple and onto the street, I was astounded to see two carriages accompanied by a cohort of legionnaires. As I turned to look for my father, I heard one of the soldiers quietly ask, "Saul, is that you?"

Whipping back around at the sound of that familiar voice, I found myself looking into the face of a Roman soldier—Justus!—smiling broadly. "No longer a little man, Saul," he said as he took three long strides and stopped directly in front of me.

I was surprised when our eyes met as he had always seemed to tower over me. Had it been only six years since I'd seen him? For a moment, the bustling street scene faded into the background as I drank in this soldier who had treated me like an equal when I was but a wide-eyed boy.

Justus waited patiently, hand out as I assimilated his presence. I shook my head and grabbed it enthusiastically. "What a delightful surprise to see you again, Justus!" I looked over at the horse closest to the street, prancing impatiently, then dropped the soldier's hand and asked, "Justus, is that …."

"Yes indeed, Saul, that is Domitius—the horse you saved from death." My old friend's eyes moistened, and so did mine as we watched the majestic stallion toss his head and tail. I moved toward the creature, and he immediately lowered his glossy, black head to nuzzle my chest.

You do remember me, you splendid creature! You do!

As I communed with Domitius, one of the other soldiers approached and said, "So, you are the Jewish kid who taught Justus how to keep our horses from lameness, eh? Congratulations on your marriage tomorrow! If you must know, I volunteered to make this trip simply for the privilege of meeting you—and thanking you. My name is Lucius." As we shook hands, I noticed that the soldier was no older than I.

Distractedly I smiled at him, but my attention was on Hannah, who was being spirited away from me by her mother and my sisters and into the first carriage. I caught only the last fragment of Lucius's animated conversation. His expression indicated that I was expected to reply.

"Lucius ... my apologies. Could you repeat—"

I was interrupted by the appearance of Justus, who moved between his soldier and me. "Lucius," he said firmly, "whatever it is you're so eager to discuss with Saul, please save it for later. For now, you must get him to the Upper City to the Rabban's home where his wedding will take place."

XXII

Although I was exhausted, I tossed and turned, unable to settle into sleep. My mind and body were wholly possessed by Hannah and thoughts of the lovemaking to come. Calculating that it was somewhere around three in the morning, I finally abandoned all efforts, threw on a cloak, and crept out of the suite which—as Gamaliel had promised—was ideally designed for a newly married couple. Beautifully appointed and containing a large and capacious bed, it was located on the third floor at the far western end of the large house. It even possessed its own private staircase.

Slowly descending, I was surprised to see the flickering light of a candle in the courtyard. Someone else was about at this ungodly hour—could it be Hannah? Instantly, I dismissed the thought; surely, she was indulging in the dreamless sleep of the innocent.

As I grew closer to the flame, I smiled at the outline of the face it illuminated. "Hello, Father," I called out, wishing that I, too, had thought to bring a candle. The courtyard was full of shadowy obstacles—all types of adornments for the next day's festivities. Sarah had outdone herself in creating a variety of flower arrangements and setting them amongst the many decorative tables and chairs.

Seeing that I made my way with difficulty, Father stood and held his candle higher, illuminating a path between the marriage canopy and the dining area set for fifty-plus guests.

We sat quietly for a few moments, but it was I who broke the silence, suddenly gripped by a deep sense of shame. Once again, I asked, "Father ... how can I thank you for all you have done for me? And how can I apologize for not doing so sooner?"

My father extended his arm and gently covered my hand with his. As he did so, I noted with shock the loose skin and dark marks of age upon it.

"My boy," he began softly, "you will soon learn how it feels to be the father of a son. We do not bring forth children to hear them say *thank you* or to see them prostrate themselves before us. We have sons so that we can join the Master of this great and mysterious universe by playing our part in the miracle of creation. We never cease to be mindful that our young do not belong to us, but to God."

Praised be Thou, O Lord our God, King of the universe who has sanctified us with His commandments and has commanded us concerning illicit relations; and has prohibited us those who are merely betrothed; but has permitted to us those lawfully married to us by chuppah and kiddushin. Blessed art thou God, who has sanctified His people Israel by chuppah and kiddushin.

Adorned in a splendid deep purple gown with matching veil, my bride stood beside me under the canopy, her right hand entwined with my left. I did not think it possible, but on this day, Hannah was more magnificent than she'd ever been. Other than in that one impetuous gesture the day before, I had not seen her adult face before this moment. Her dark hair shimmered in the sunshine, competing with the gold jewels plaiting her curls. Her long-lashed, magnificent, gold-flecked eyes caressed my face until I felt as if I were drowning in her gaze.

So, God created man in His own image,
in the image of God He created him;
male and female he created them.

Rabban Gamaliel's voice rose as he declared, "Be fertile and multiply!"

As if from a distance, I heard shouts, clapping, and cheers … but I could not tear my gaze away from Hannah.

XXIII

❦

Hannah and I were scheduled to depart for Tarsus the following day. The past six days had felt like an idyllic dream, one that I feared awakening from. Reason and the banality of the practical simmered at the edges of my mind. *Happiness like this cannot endure; it is incompatible with our lives of sacrifice and toil. This has been ordained since the beginning.*

I watched my wife sleep beside me, her lovely face unlined, her sensuous lips upturned in a shadow of a smile. As I observed her gentle breathing, I pondered the words of Genesis I had known by heart since a very young boy:

The Lord God said, "It is not good for the man to be alone. I will make a helper suitable for him."

Now the Lord God had formed out of the ground all the wild animals and all the birds in the sky. He brought them to the man to see what he would name them; and whatever the man called each living creature, that was its name.

So the man gave names to all the livestock, the birds in the sky and all the wild animals. But for Adam, no suitable helper was found.

So the Lord God caused the man to fall into a deep sleep; and while he was sleeping, he took one of the man's ribs and then closed up the place with flesh.

Then the Lord God made a woman from the rib he had taken out of the man, and he brought her to the man.

The man said, "This is now bone of my bones and flesh of my flesh; she shall be called 'woman,' for she was taken out of man."

That is why a man leaves his father and mother and is united to his wife, and they become one flesh.

Adam and his wife were both naked, and they felt no shame.

Reverently, I tasted the heft of the words in my mind and heart. In truth, Hannah had become "bone of my bones, flesh of my flesh." I remained Saul, yet I knew we were one—and that I was far more than the man I had been just six days earlier. I was the same, yet altered inexplicably.

Casting my mind back to my school days, I recalled that occasionally, one of my fellow students would speak or even cry about his loneliness. Although I would try to offer words of comfort, I am sure I appeared cold and distant—for isolation was something I had never understood. In fact, I had always treasured my solitude, going all the way back to my early years of goatherding.

I smiled to myself as I ruminated about my new life with Hannah—the intensity of my desire, my physical need, and the plethora of emotions unleashed by its satisfaction. Hannah had proved a robustly eager lover, but this sense of being *more* because of her presence in my life was wholly unexpected. I'd never dreamed of feeling filled up in this way because I hadn't known of the space she'd come to fill.

A memory drifted into my consciousness. Rabban Gamaliel was teaching us about King Leonidas and the infamous last day of the War of Thermopylae. Arrogantly, I only half-listened because I considered myself an expert on the Spartan King and his primary warrior, Dienekes. But Gamaliel was not discussing the odds or tactics of the battle; instead, he was discussing love.

Knowing his question would catch me off guard, Rabban asked, "Saul, how many words are there in Greek for *love*?"

Uncharacteristically, I stammered, having no answer on the tip of my tongue.

Abruptly, my teacher turned to his son. "Simeon, how many words are there in Latin for love?" he asked.

"Just two, Rabban," my friend responded confidently. "And they arise from just one root."

"And how many in Greek?"

"Eight, Rabban." Simeon proceeded to list and define all eight words, focusing on *philautia*, unique to the Greek, meaning *the love of oneself that is essential to the health of both mind and body.*

"And in Hebrew?" Rabban persisted.

"There are ten Hebrew words for love, Rabban," replied Simeon, rattling off and defining each one in turn.

That discussion had taken place over five years ago—well before my marriage. At the time, I'd thought it a waste of time—trivial—to study such words, though I never forgot one of them or its specific meaning. But now, as I gazed down at my dozing bride, I finally comprehended the brilliant meaning of Rabban's lesson. He had taken time and energy to teach us the many ways to describe a state without boundaries. Clearly, the reality of love—its immensity—was such that no one word in any human language could explain it adequately.

XXIV

I squinted in the brilliant sunlight and smiled politely at Rabban Gamaliel, Sarah, Simeon, and Rabban's servant Bilhah. I was feeling dazed and more than a little sorrowful as my wife, and I emerged—abruptly and painfully—into the world. Hannah, on the other hand, flitted from one to the other, pressing her hands to their faces and murmuring endearments.

Nothing seems to perturb this woman, I thought to myself. *Hannah adapts to her circumstances, while I stand here like a stick.*

My wife and I had been entwined for six days, only rarely coming out to join the other wedding guests. Bilhah had treated us like royalty, entering our suite only when we stepped outside for toilet and hygiene. Each time she did, she left a sumptuous dish for our nourishment along with generous draughts of water and wine. She was now engrossed in packing a large container of food and drink to sustain us on our journey back to Tarsus.

Bilhah's name—which means bashful—suited her, for she was timid and blushed easily whenever anyone spoke to her. She was most comfortable with her head down, working, as she was now.

Leaving everyone embroiled in conversation, I walked through the courtyard door and onto the street, where Justus and several of his soldiers awaited us. "*Salve*, Justus!" I said, regarding the scarlet plume on his helmet with surprise. "I must have missed your promotion to the rank of centurion! Congratulations!" I knew my family was to travel with a portion of Justus's cavalry unit. It was now clear who would be leading it.

My friend grinned and nodded, not bothering to hide his pride. "Yes, Saul," he said, "the Tribune promoted me after our last battle in Germanica." Once the words had left his lips, his smile faded, and he turned away, suddenly focused on one of his soldiers.

He must be returning in his mind to the horrors of the battlefield, I thought. *Perhaps even to the loss of beloved comrades.* I stood silently, watching him. What could I possibly say? Although I had not and most likely would never experience war, I imagined the toll it must take—the nightmares Justus and his ilk must suffer.

After a few moments, he turned back to look at me. "Maximillian was killed in that battle," he said gravely.

Shocked, aghast, I closed my eyes as if in doing so, I could ward off the knowledge of his death. Maximillian was the centurion who had looked down from the Garden of Olives after our harrowing ascent through the Ben-Horons Pass and whispered, "Jerusalem, surely this is a city befitting the worship of the Gods." At the time, it had felt like a blessing.

I opened my eyes and regarded Justus, whose eyes betrayed his distance from the moment. Rocked by the terrifying fragility of men's lives, I could picture Maximillian clearly: powerful, muscular, with handsome features that softened into tenderness as he looked down upon the glory of Jerusalem.

Closing my eyes once again, I whispered a prayer for the soulful centurion.

Taking a couple of steps to close the distance between us, Justus gripped my shoulder hard. "Saul," he said urgently, "I must tell you that Maximillian died saving my life. Were it not for him, I would not be here. My horse had been fatally speared … I was on the ground, reaching desperately for my javelin, which had disappeared in the mud. Two of the Germanicus mercenaries rode up and were about to throw everything they had at me when Maximillian appeared out of nowhere. He killed the first one easily, but the second threw his spear, connecting with my champion's neck. I watched as a geyser of bright blood spurted from him, yet he managed to launch his gladius."

These last words, Justus spoke so softly that I had to strain to listen. I could feel the tears springing to my eyes, but I don't think he noticed. His gaze was clearly directed inward, trained on the terrible memory of that day.

Shaking his head as if to clear the vision away, he continued, "In the beginning, for us soldiers, it is all about the Empire and the Emperor; the glory of war and of giving our lives for Rome." He narrowed his eyes as if trying to see a great distance. "But, after just one battle … the lakes of blood, the screams of dying men, we learn quickly that it is for one another that we fight. For our brothers. The Empire? The glory of Rome?" A dry, sardonic chuckle seeped through his compressed lips. "*The Emperor?*" Blinking rapidly and shaking his head once more, Justus exhaled a long whistling breath, and his smile returned but seemed forced. "So … you are a married man now, Saul. Please accept my congratulations to you and your wife."

As if on cue, the door opened, and there she stood, beaming. "Are we leaving now, my love?" she asked.

"Momentarily, my dear. I just need to go pick up our satchels and Bilhah's crate of food."

Smiling first at me and then at Justus, Hannah said to him, "I hope you and your men are hungry, sir. I suspect there is enough in there for a legion!"

XXV

The Road to Tarsus

At the abrupt halt of the coach, I toppled off the wooden bench of the carriage and Hannah followed, landing on top of me. She had spent the previous few hours dozing with her head on my shoulder, now and then commenting on something I said. This shook us both from our languor.

After scrambling upright and making sure my wife was all right—if a bit shaken up—I stood and opened the carriage door. Immediately, a man shouted in our direction, "Do NOT come out! Stay inside the coach and get down on the floor!"

Who had called out so urgently? Not Justus; the voice was unfamiliar. Nevertheless, I pulled the door closed, grabbed Hannah, and we dropped again to the floor. In an instant came a series of agonized screams, shrieks, howls, and the clamor of frenzied activity. I judged the commotion to be coming from the front and left of the carriage. Improbably, it sounded like an attack of wild animals ... or could it have been the horses making those ungodly sounds?

After what was probably only a few minutes but felt like far longer, Justus opened the carriage door. He held a blood-ied javelin. "Forgive the uproar," he said breathlessly. "A pack of huge and hungry wolves must have decided we'd make a nice main course." Seeing Hannah's eyes widen in terror, he glanced at the javelin and the blood dripping onto the ground below, mumbled an apology, and stashed it behind his back. "Saul, you can come out if you'd like, but I suggest that your wife stay where she is, rather than view the carnage." His grimace thinned out his full lips. "We had to put down two of the horses who bolted at the appearance of the pack. The wolves brought them down by shredding their legs. I am sure you heard their screams."

At the thought of it, and of the necessary destruction of the beloved animals, we both shook our heads.

I watched as Hannah bit the inside of her lip and attempted—but failed—to smile. "Thank you, Justus," she said, unfailingly polite. "I have no need to see them." Looking up at me, she said, "I am fine, Saul. Go ahead and look around, but I would rather not hear about it."

I hesitated, unsure whether I should leave her.

"Go," she repeated.

Closest to the rear of the coach lay the body of what must have been the alpha female. She looked to be almost seventy kilograms—one of the most enormous wolves I had ever seen of either gender. A few times back in Tarsus, Eli and I had seen these beasts skulking around, but they'd been half the size. Our Canaan dogs had chased them away with ease.

Looking at the carcass, I thought of Channah, the alpha of the guard dogs tasked with protecting our newborn goats. She was fiercely loyal and would have died protecting those kids. I did not think she would have had a chance among these monsters.

Justus had disappeared somewhere, but his next in command, Fabius, said, "It will take us a while to clean up." He nodded toward a grievous tableau off toward the west. Two groups of mounted soldiers were dragging the corpses of two horses toward the river. "We would like to make it as difficult as possible for the remainder of this pack to survive." Answering my unspoken question, he added, "Some of the men insist that they have seen wolves this big before, but I think they are exaggerating." With a glance toward the soldiers, he added, "I guess I should get back there and help."

I watched him ride away and then went to check on the four horses pulling our coach. Surprisingly, they were relatively calm—a bit skittish, but then, so was I. The smell of death hung heavily in the still air as I stood rubbing the ears of the lead horse—my beloved Domitius—and looking out over the beautiful forested plain. I mused about the strangeness of the wolf attack. The only explanation I could think of for such aggressive behavior was severe hunger. Maybe there were cubs out in those woods.

According to Fabius, we were about thirty-two kilometers south of Antioch, where we would spend the night. I had never been to Antioch but felt as if I had, for our tentmaking business had numerous customers there. Soon, I would begin to take on a lot of the traveling for the company, to lessen the burden upon Father and Shimon.

Father had often spoken of the beauty of Antioch. Its unusual topography, carved by the river Orontes out of the plain between two mountain ranges, had bewitched him. Whether due to flooding or plan, a part of the city was wholly encircled by the river and could be reached only by boat. I looked forward to seeing it.

Domitius's flank twitched in sheer pleasure under my hands. I had moved past the harness and was massaging his side when I sensed movement behind me. Turning, I saw Justus whispering with Hannah, who was leaning out of the carriage. Every now and then, one of them glanced at me. Although I was curious as to what they might be talking about, I continued my ministrations, enjoying the almost meditative motion of my hands on the stallion's body. I had missed this silent communion with animals and felt pleasure at the thought that I would soon be spending peaceful, quiet days with the goatherds and horses at our farm in Tarsus.

XXVI

Outskirts of Antioch

Justus had merely laughed at my offer to cool down the horses for the night upon our arrival at a large and quite beautiful tavern. "Saul, you are a married man now, not a child. I have plenty of men who can take good care of Domitius and the others."

He and I had been standing outside, watching the soldiers fight a sudden driving rain while leading the horses into the barn. Neither of us minded the soaking after what we had experienced earlier that day. Turning to walk into the tavern to find my wife, I heard Justus shout, "But thank you for the offer!"

Refreshed after a bath and some rest, Hannah, Fabius, Justus, and I sat at a rectangular wooden table not far from the stone kitchen, from which emanated the enticing fragrance of grilled meats and warm bread. The other soldiers had filled most of the tables in the back of the large tavern and were contently savoring their first chalices of wines. The inn, which sat about fifteen kilometers south of the city, was enormous and almost what you'd call *opulent*, with mosaic floors and stone fireplaces. The effect was gracious and welcoming.

Lifting up his cup of wine, Justus exclaimed, "Saul and Hannah! May the gods bless you and give you many sons!"

I smiled at this soldier who had become a good friend

and bowed my head, "Thank you, Justus. Not merely for your good wishes but for so effectively safeguarding us on our journey back to Tarsus." He and Fabius simply nodded at my comment. No one had any desire to revisit the horror of the wolf attack, or what might have happened had the soldiers not acted so swiftly.

We all sipped our wine and enjoyed the warmth of the place and the pleasurable sound of conversations at the other tables. The patter of rain pelting the roof added yet another dimension to our feelings of gratitude for our haven.

Once the platters of food arrived, the only sound was of satisfied people enjoying delicious and restorative food. I had noticed a glance between Justus and the young waitress as she cleared the table, but had thought nothing of it until she reappeared with a cake and eighteen candles.

I looked over at my wife as it was placed before me. She raised both hands to her mouth in sheer delight at the festive surprise she had planned. The custom was new to our experience, but we both knew that the Greeks and Romans celebrated birthdays in this way.

"So, this is what you two were whispering about earlier!" I said in mock accusation.

Both Justus and Hannah laughed and nodded enthusiastically.

I inhaled deeply and blew out the candles, in the manner of the pagans. As I divided up the cake, I said, "Hannah, maybe we should do this again for your birthday. What an entertaining way to commemorate the occasion!"

"Saul, are you asleep?"

I think Hannah knew that I was not, as I had spent a restless few hours trying to get comfortable. "Yes," I replied mockingly, "are you?"

Giggling softly, she moved closer and asked, "Saul, are

you anxious at the prospect of being back in Tarsus?"

I thought about it for a few moments and decided the answer was yes—though I hadn't been aware of this feeling until Hannah asked the question. Quite suddenly, I felt vulnerable. "Yes, my love ... I suppose I am a bit anxious," I replied finally. "Why do you ask?"

It was Hannah's turn to pause. "Because I would be, were I you," she answered carefully.

I chuckled at this child-woman, wise beyond her years. "You would, would you?" *Why am I taking this condescending tone? I wondered, and why do I feel so defensive?*

"I ... did not ask the question to annoy you, Saul," she said stiffening.

Not wanting to fan any flames of discord between us, I lay there thinking about this woman, this *flesh of my flesh, bone of my bone*. I was well aware that there were parts of myself that I had always guarded, kept private, for one reason only. I'd never wanted to suffer the indignities and shame of my childhood again. I would do anything to bury the jeering cries of the Greek boys who'd chased me, and the disappointment—whether real or imagined—etched into my father's face after my error in the synagogue. I knew I had walled off a part of myself so that I would never again feel the pain of ridicule and rejection. But, in doing so, I had lost something precious. If I could not burn away the remnants of my shame, it threatened to stand as a barrier between my new wife and me.

Hannah's being was so familiar to me and yet so alien, her thoughts and mannerisms so wholly unlike my own. She seemed to have access to a source of knowledge that I could never reach. I thought back to the time in Gamaliel's courtyard when she had been so effortlessly gracious to Rabban and his wife while I had stood there. And then I cast my mind back even further, to the day of my seventh birthday and the long walk back from the synagogue. Though only five at the time, Hannah had refused to leave my side. Even then, she had been able to soothe my feelings, deflect the anger I projected like the hot rays of the sun. Only God could have created such a creature.

"My dearest Hannah, flesh of my flesh, " I said, instantly feeling her begin to relax at my side. "You must be patient with this simpleton you have chosen to love and marry. You see, I am unaccustomed to having a resident in my heart and psyche, one I love more than life itself." I encircled her with my arms and pulled her close. "Now ... tell me why you would be anxious about returning to Tarsus if you were me." This time, I said it as if I genuinely wanted to know—and I did. This wife of mine might very well be able to perceive in me feelings that I could not recognize—or refused to.

Propping herself up on one elbow, Hannah looked down at me, her long-lashed eyes keen, her expression somber. "Because my husband, the home you left as a child, is no longer."

She paused while I weighed her words. I had not stopped to think about how different my home would seem to me. Mother was gone, Esther and my sisters married. The constant pandemonium of my boyhood was a thing of the past.

"Saul, you have spent the last six years in scholarly pursuit—dwelling in quite heady circles. Now, that has ended, and, in one sense, you are coming home. But in another, far more significant way, you are simply moving on, having left your home forever at age twelve. Your return to Tarsus will be as a business partner to your father and mine." Her lovely mouth turned upward into a shy smile. "And as the head of a new family—our family. It is for those reasons that I imagine I might be a bit apprehensive if I were you."

XXVII

Tarsus

It was spring, and the goats were kidding. I had forgotten how many places I needed to be at that time of year. Our business had quadrupled in my absence, and we had more than 300 employees, most of whom were strangers to me. Twice I had approached my father and Shimon about creating new supervisory positions, but each conversation had been put aside for more pressing matters.

Thankfully, Eli was still there—well into his seventies but still as agile as a man half his age. We worked together as if I had never been gone. Goats will eat almost anything, including twigs, sticks, and desiccated weeds, but we had learned that their hair becomes far more pliable on a diet of mostly grass. That meant moving them around the pastures continuously, which we did by working in groups of four with exceptional help from Channah, the alpha female of our Canaan dogs. Fortunately, our farmland was on the rainy side of Cilicia, so the grass grew back quickly.

It fell to Eli and me to train new workers, and we did so efficiently. One day, I was mentoring two Greek youths under the age of twenty. I had just finished pointing out to one of them—Ammiel—the signs that a doe was about to give birth when I saw a woman approaching us at a trot. Fearing she might trip on one of the small rodent holes in the grass, I took off toward her, reaching her just as she came through the main gate. "Miriam," I panted, "is it time?"

"Yes, Sir ... her water has broken." Our young servant could barely get the words out. Her chest was heaving, and the hood of her robe was askew, revealing a tangled mass of light-brown curly hair.

Our house was at least a kilometer from where I had been working, but in under ten minutes, I was tearing through the courtyard and bursting through the door. "HANNAH!" I cried out, racing upstairs. She was not in our bed, as I had expected. Now I was panicked in addition to being breathless. Again, I shouted, "HANNAH!"

"Yes, Saul," came her voice floating up to me from the other side of the house. "I am here—in the kitchen."

As I scurried back down the staircase, through the courtyard, and into the main house, I tried to control my fear. I had been anxious about this birth for many weeks. Each day, Hannah's girth had seemed to increase by meters. When looking at her, I could not help but wonder how on earth she would be able to bring that enormous infant into this world safely. On the occasions when she caught me staring, she would laugh—a bell-like peal that usually warmed my heart but now irritated me.

When the time came, it would be just the two of us as the midwives lived in the city. I knew almost all there was to know about delivering baby goats, but Hannah? My wife seemed oblivious to the dangers I knew could happen.

Father had built an extension on our Tarsus house for my family and me, the year I asked Hannah to marry. It was similar to that of Gamaliel's in that there was a separate stairway from the courtyard up to the second floor, which contained both bedrooms and sitting rooms, and afforded us a great deal of privacy. The house had been spacious before, but now it seemed huge as I raced down both sets of stairs, past my father's bedroom, and on into the kitchen at the back of the house.

Hannah looked calmly at me as I burst into the kitchen, panting, open-mouthed at the sight of my wife. "I'm sorry Miriam frightened you," she said. "I'm perfectly fine. She is just a young girl and has no experience in such matters ... I believe she got a little overwrought when my water broke, but I assure you, it is all in the normal course of things."

"My darling, may I remind you that Miriam is exactly your age?" I pointed out, wondering for the hundredth time where my wife got all of her worldly wisdom.

Tiny beads of sweat lined the top of her face as Hannah pounded grains of wheat into a fine flour. "We are almost out of bread," she explained, her face radiant, "so I decided to—"

She stopped short and grimaced, clearly experiencing a contraction. One hand gripped the ledge of the stone counter where she worked, the other went to her abdomen. Her hand looked child-like against the enormous protuberance of her belly. As I watched, more perspiration appeared on her reddening face.

Trying to look calm though my heart hammered in my chest, I ambled over to her as if it seemed the most reasonable thing in the world to be making bread in the early stages of childbirth. Before I could offer a word or caress, Miriam burst into the kitchen, panting, hair disheveled. "You are making bread? Now?" she shrieked.

"Miriam," I interjected as evenly as I could manage, "Would you please start to boil some water and gather some towels?" The instant she turned away to do as I asked, I put my arms around my wife, lifted her, and carried her up the long stairway to our private quarters at the back of my father's house.

XXIII

As I watched Hannah and our newborn son David sleep, I wondered if there could possibly be any more magnificent sight in this world. Our boy's head and shoulders were enormous, or, at least they seemed so to me. I knew the pain of the delivery had been excruciating, yet Hannah had uttered barely a sound—just kept murmuring, over and over, "I cannot wait to see you, my son." Her joy when, finally, I placed him at her breast was palpable, her expression incandescent.

From the moment she'd known she was with child, Hannah had insisted that he be named David after my father. This had surprised and pleased me no end, as had her certainty about his sex. I was growing accustomed to my wife's foreshadowings and learning to trust them.

Father's reaction to his grandson's name frankly astounded me.

"I … we … would like your permission to name your grandson David—after you," Hannah said to my father one night over a dinner she'd prepared especially for the occasion. We'd decided that she should be the one to ask him, and I knew at that moment it had been the right thing to do.

Placing his silverware down carefully, my father bowed his head as if in prayer. When he raised his face a moment later, I could see that it was wet with tears. Slowly and with effort, he stood. I restrained myself from helping him, knowing that he detested any acknowledgment of his advancing age and infirmities. As he made his way toward Hannah, she and I avoided looking at each other for fear our emotions would get the better of us.

"Daughter, you cannot know how happy you are making me," Father said quietly, his voice quivering a little and his face aglow. Had I ever seen him this emotional? I thought back to something Hannah had said about him when explaining to me her reason for choosing the name: "Saul, your father must be anxious about the tribe of Benjamin … about his family name. Your sisters have given him grandsons, but they have the names of other men. I think he needs to know the family name will go on. I think it will give him a reason to go on himself."

At the time, I'd thought Hannah was being a bit overly emotional; but now, watching my father embrace his only daughter-in-law, I saw and appreciated the depth of her insight.

From that day forward, my father seemed to grow younger. There was a new lightness in his step and vitality in his spirit. Even his back, stooped by years of labor, appeared to straighten by inches.

During the next monthly meeting at the farm, Shimon interrupted my entreaty that some of the employees needed far more training than they were currently getting and that a reorganization was called for.

"Saul," he said, his palm upright, "I agree with you. We will do this. You work out the details, including the names of the men you want to promote and the pay you suggest. But I must ask your father what his secret is. Since you and Hannah moved in with him, he looks younger with each passing week."

Casting a glance at me as if for permission, Father shouted, "Shimon! We are soon to be grandparents! You and I and …" Looking for all the world like a guilty little boy, he continued, "I hope you do not mind, my dear friend, but they are going to name their son …" He could not get his own name out for fear of choking up.

"Saul, Saul! Come out, come out, wherever you are!"

The moment I heard that voice, I ran through the courtyard and out to the street, then embraced my oldest sister so enthusiastically that I took her breath away.

Once again, our home was overflowing with revelry. My sisters, Esther, Anat, Mikhal, and Rachel, had arrived with their families for David's *brit malah* three days earlier. Esther now had five children—three girls and two boys—but slipped instantly back into her role as oldest sister to me and, by extension, Hannah and even Father. Although the years and childbearing had taken a toll on her body, Esther's nature was wholly unchanged. Overflowing with love and concern for everyone but herself, she had not stopped working since her arrival. She'd also managed to delegate a variety of kitchen work to her younger sisters—from making bread to preparing the lamb for the upcoming celebration.

Including the numerous friends and associates from the synagogue and our business, the number of people in the house, courtyard, and milling around outside must have been in the hundreds—but Hannah and David remained the stars of the occasion. Although our son was a mere eight days old, he had not uttered a single cry; he merely regarded whoever held him with enormous, unblinking, dark-brown eyes that seemed to reflect the wisdom of the universe. I myself could get lost in my son's regard.

When the time came for the *brit,* everything was ready. As Shimon and Father lit the Havdalah candle, all conversation ceased, and silence descended like a cloud over the hundreds of people gathered inside and outside the house. Each member of the crowd was well aware that this ritual marked the beginning of the eighth day—the day God taught us how to make light. While God Himself had begun creation with "Let there be light!" we celebrated the eighth day as the human contribution to the creation, marking our creative partnership with the Lord.

As the scripture informs us, Adam and Eve had sinned and were exiled from the Garden, but God's mercy permitted them to spend an extra day there—*shabbat*—before their exile. As that day ended and they faced banishment into the darkness, the Lord showed them how to make light. For that reason, the *Mishkan*—God's sanctuary—was created on the eighth day: a space of forty cubits containing the Creator of the Universe.

It was as if I could hear the whispers of my desert-dwelling ancestors as they followed the Sanctuary and Moses, and "brought willing offerings to the Lord, every man and woman whose heart made them willing to bring for all manner of work which the Lord had commanded."

Abounding with the privilege of my Hebrew faith and rabbinical training, I took my place as the father of the child, in front of the table where David lay. I closed my eyes and prayed:

And God said unto Abraham: 'And as for thee, thou shalt keep My covenant, thou, and thy seed after thee throughout their generations. This is My covenant ... every male among you shall be circumcised. And ye shall be circumcised in the flesh of your foreskin, and it shall be a token of a covenant betwixt Me and you. And he that is eight days old shall be circumcised among you, every male throughout your generations ... And the uncircumcised male who is not circumcised in the flesh of his foreskin shall be cut off from his people; he hath broken My covenant.

David's legs were splayed apart, and Hannah stood at his head, holding his arms; Father and Shimon stood at each side, holding his legs. The enormous eyes of my child stared unwaveringly into mine. With my left hand, I straightened his tiny penis, grabbed the sharp knife so quickly that I cut my index finger, then promptly pierced his foreskin with the point of my knife, made the cut, and applied the ring to the top of his penis. It was over in less than twenty seconds and, while just one of us was screaming, both of us were bleeding.

Within minutes, David was contently nursing at Hannah's breast. The celebration began anew and continued for an entire week.

Father and Shimon had agreed to the list I'd compiled of trusted men who might serve as supervisors of smaller groups of our three hundred employees. Eli, at seventy-five, led the largest group of fifty goatherders, and so on. The reorganization permitted me to assume the travel duties formerly fulfilled by my father and Shimon, allowing them to spend more time with Hannah and our boy.

The weeks became months and then years, and suddenly, I faced my twenty-eighth birthday—a day that began like any other.

XXIX

Mamertine Prison

For many years—decades, in fact—I'd fought to suppress memories of my ten years as a husband to Hannah and father to David and our unborn second son. They had been years of happiness, yes, but also of frustration, uncertainty, anxiety—the typical responses to life as we all know it.

It takes no more than the blink of an eye to become complacent; to expect that each new day will replicate the previous. Succumbing to such a feeling, I soon permitted the daily tasks, challenges, and occasional crises of my busy life to eclipse the joy of family life: our son's mastery of walking, for example. Similarly, consumed by the prospect of meeting a new customer in Antioch, I failed to notice the early signs of pregnancy in my wife.

As most of us do, I took for granted the fact that my wife and I would grow old together, welcome our grandchildren into this world, and watch as our own children grew white-haired. This is the way of things. We trust in our youth and fidelity to God, believing our relationship with our Lord to be contractual: If we pray and follow His laws, He will keep us and those we love safe and unharmed. For many—including Shimon, Leah, and my father—that is how it came to pass. They were into their eighth or ninth decades of life when the earthquake struck. Not so, my bride, my children, and myself.

What choice had I, after the cataclysm, but to move on, enshrouding my lost life as best I could in the mists of the distant past? I accomplished this so well that most came to believe me to be an icon of celibacy. At times, I succeeded in convincing myself that those years were but a dream I'd had and awakened from.

That I suffered not even a scratch amidst such utter devastation seemed an absurdity, an irony of the most epic proportions. I tormented myself with my belief that it would all have been different had I stayed home; that I could have saved my family.

I wish I could tell you that I thanked the Lord for each day, each minute I'd been granted with them. Or that there had never been moments during our lives together when I'd wished for solitude or the return to my carefree life as a student.

When I kissed my wife that last time, it was hurried, perfunctory. I knew the journey to the market would take most of the day, and I barely looked at her face, anxious to get started. When I knelt down to kiss the top of David's head, he begged to come along with me. I smiled indulgently, but my answer was no, that he had to stay to take care of his mother. My son simply nodded and raced back into the house.

I wish I could say that I understood why it all happened the way it did—or that I understand it even now. I cannot. What I can say with certainty is this: had I not lost everything and everyone, including myself, I would not have descended into the depths of the abyss. And it was from out of that abyss that Salvation plucked me up into Life.

XXX

Jerusalem

We were in the Chamber of Hewn Stones. Instead of the jubilation I should have felt at sitting among the sages as the youngest member ever admitted to the august group known as the Sanhedrin, I felt hollow. It was as if the gorge that had split Tarsus cut through my chest. I could not recall the last time I had slept because closing my eyes meant dreaming, and dreaming meant re-experiencing the stench and sounds of death. So much death.

My pain and torpor rendered me incapable of following the discussion amongst the seventy-odd other members of the Sanhedrin. Although I had been in Jerusalem listening to these proceedings for close to a week, I had gleaned only a few facts.

There had been a crucifixion—of yet another pretender who claimed to be the Messiah. The act had caused more conflict than I could recall witnessing among the Sanhedrin. This charlatan called Jesus had been dead for over two months, and yet, somehow, he was causing problems from the grave. A handful of his followers, all Galileans, claimed he had risen from the dead.

Laughable.
Moronic.

But neither Caiaphas nor Annas was amused, nor were Nicodemus, Josephus, or any of the others. Even Gamaliel was subdued.

Although I yearned to speak up, I refrained from doing so. To my colleagues, I remained a student, beloved but, in their eyes, still a child. Beyond that, I feared that my agitated state and lack of sleep might keep me from speaking coherently. To earn the attention of these elders, coherence was but one of a very long list of requisites.

It was as if a weight pressed down upon this body of men, stifling everyone's spirits. The lively debates and contentious discussions I'd imagined taking place while a student at the Temple were nowhere to be heard. Instead, long moments of silence followed reports of "sightings" by various Galileans. At first, I figured that these men were growing older—as all men do—and less full of the zeal and passion of youth. But as the hours wore on, that explanation would not stand.

Distinct impressions of something besides weariness came to silence my tongue.

Fear.

I knew these men. A few of them—most especially Gamaliel—I knew even better than my own father. At least I thought I did. After all, I had studied under them with the strict adherence of a pubescent zealot. After six years of study, I had gotten so that I could predict my mentors' reactions to things with uncanny accuracy—especially those of Caiaphas. I now regarded him as he entered slowly and ceremoniously from the inner sanctuary and traversed the length of the outer temple, finally stopping in front of the gathering. The silence as all waited for him to speak was broken only by the occasional chirp of a courageous sparrow.

He was clad in his full ceremonial garb. The twelve precious stones on the breastplate attached to his *ephod*—the beautifully woven violet, scarlet, and blue garment embroidered with figures of gold—caused me to squint in the sunlight. As I attempted to focus my gaze, the morning sun transformed the green, red, and yellow jewels into a rainbow of fire.

"We must convince our people that the Galileans stole into the tomb during the night and removed the body," the High Priest declared. He paused for several moments to let the tension build higher, then shouted, "WE MUST PUT A STOP TO THESE INSANE STORIES OF A RISEN CHRIST!"

Murmurs of assent sounded throughout the room. From one corner, I heard, "Arrest the Galileans!"

Another voice shouted, "FIND THEM AND STONE THEM TO DEATH!"

Others soon chimed in, creating a chorus raised against the evil and darkness these men saw creeping over their faith.

To me, they sounded like small children rebuffing imaginary monsters.

This was a brand of fear I had never experienced in holy men. Unaccountably, I began to wake. The disorientation and helplessness that had gripped me began to loosen and fall away. Suddenly, I felt more alert, confident, and aware than I had been since the earthquake. In that instant, I knew what my purpose was.

This is why my life was spared ... to act on behalf of these holy men who are too old and too feeble to do what must be done ... for the faith of Abraham, Jacob, and David. This was the war for which I had trained my entire life. I would lead the fight against these blasphemers.

I stood up. But, just as I was about to shout into the jumbled sound of voices, a hand grabbed my arm in a grip of iron.

Gamaliel stood beside me like a pillar of stone.

"Come with me now, Saul."

"But ... Rabban ... I can help! I know—"

"Follow me now, Saul."

It did not seem possible that this elderly man should so easily overpower me, but he did.

Still in his grip, I allowed him to propel me out of the hall, into the courtyard, and out of the Temple.

XXXI

"Why did you stop me, Rabban? Finally, I understand why I alone survived! The hand of God reached into my life to take away my wife, my boy, everyone and everything I love, leaving only me. For hours, I lay in the rubble of my existence, begging to join them in extinction. But now, sitting among this crowd of old, tired men, I see why I was spared the death that enveloped Tarsus. Don't you see, Rabban? The elders cannot deal with these zealots. They need someone young and strong, filled with the zeal of the God of Abraham, Isaac, and Jacob."

Blustering, full of righteous indignation, my diatribe had echoed ironically within the magnificent edifice through which we passed—a place so wondrous that I had dropped to my knees in awe the first time I had viewed it from the Mount of Olives. Now, I took no notice of the splendor surrounding me. "No one is better prepared than I to take down these Galileans and their false messiah!" I shouted at Gamaliel's back—for he had not slowed down to listen to my harangue.

As I raced to keep up with him, he moved quickly down the semi-circular steps to the Court of the Israelites, then through the colossal archway known as Nicanor's Gate to the Women's Court. The years had been kind to my teacher, and his strides were long and graceful; his long robe flapped rhythmically with each step. From the back, he could easily have been mistaken for a man of my years.

Realizing that Gamaliel was headed down to the Beautiful Gate and out to the streets of the old city, I fell silent and quickened my own pace in an attempt to keep up. I found myself breathing hard from the exertion and perspiring despite the cool evening breeze.

Gamaliel's home in the Upper City was not far from Caiaphas's palace. That seemed to be where he was heading, but in the fog of my mind, nothing looked familiar—not even the Temple. I distrusted my ability to find my way on my own, so I knew I'd best not lose sight of the old man. When, finally, I caught up to him, it was in the elaborately decorated hallway of the Beautiful Gate. As I watched, he paused for just a moment, and I heard the tinkle of two coins hitting the tin cup of a seated beggar I'd not seen or heard, though he was well within my field of view.

Gamaliel regarded me with neither judgment nor pity—a mercy for which I was profoundly grateful. The thought that he might show me compassion or empathy inspired nothing but an all-too-familiar emptiness.

Gamaliel understood that—like many in Jerusalem—I had lost everyone precious to me in the earthquake, as well the most prosperous tent-making business in that part of the world. His gray-blue eyes, as he turned them on me, had lost none of their inner light. His countenance was gracious and gentle as if he might bestow praise rather than imprecations—and this pierced my very soul. For a moment, the years rolled away, and I recalled the love this man had always shown me. Gamaliel was a born teacher, his eyes harboring the wisdom of the universe. Trapped now within their regard, I felt the energy of my rage drain away, and the deep darkness rush back in, threatening to destroy me.

Saying nothing, we continued at a slower pace. The long, silent walk to Upper Jerusalem should have calmed me by adding to my exhaustion. Instead, my mind seethed with the Spartan stories from my youth. I imagined myself as Xerxes, the Persian king whose soldiers destroyed the noblest army the world had ever seen; then as Dienekes, King Leonidas's famed Spartan commander during the week-long battle in which the Spartans held off more than a million Persians.

My childhood tutor, Pylenor, would have beamed to read my thoughts. My recall of those horrific battles was flawless—especially the final battle of Thermopylae. Vividly, I envisioned the exhausted Spartans catching sight of the Persian King Xerxes's Immortals marching through the Narrow Gates, resplendent in their golden skull crowns. Many wore eye kohl and rouge, their half helmets exposing throat, jaw, neck, and face. Each warrior was more resplendent than the one beside him, all in their purple and scarlet silk tunics and sleeveless coats of mail. Their wicker shields extended from shoulder to groin, but most remarkable of all was the abundance of gold amulets, bracelets, and brooches each one wore. It was as if the army were marching toward a banquet rather than a battle to the death. Obsessively, I thought of the question that Dienekes had repeatedly asked of his loyal Spartan warriors: "*What is the opposite of fear?*"

But it was the severely wounded King Leonidas's final words to the 100 Spartans that echoed most powerfully in my memory as we approached our destination:

> *If we had withdrawn from these Gates today, dear brothers, no matter what excesses of valor we had performed in these last days of battle, would have been considered defeat. A failure which would have affirmed what Xerxes wishes all of Greece to believe: That it is futile to resist the Persians and all their millions. But by*

our deaths here with honor, in the face of these impossible odds, we transform defeat into victory. With our blood, we sow courage in the hearts of our allies and the brothers of the armies left behind. They are the ones who will ultimately emerge victorious.

It was never our fate to vanquish the enemy but instead, what we knew when we embraced our wives and children: to stand and die. Our allied brothers are on the road home now. We must cover their withdrawal; otherwise, the Persian cavalry will roll our comrades down before they've covered ten miles. If we can hold for a few hours more, our brothers will be safe.

We'd made it to the Upper City and were passing the agora where all manner of vendors competed for the attention of the tourists. I had been so self-absorbed that I had not noticed their raucous shouts and chuckled at the irony. *Here I was, in sackcloth and ashes, cursing the day I was born, surrounded by hundreds of Jews thinking only about saving a few shekels on the fish for their evening meal.*

I had forgotten what the city was like during Passover and the weeks that followed. In that world at that time, commerce was king.

XXXII

The sight of Gamaliel's house, all clad in pristine white marble, still impressed, although I had spent six years studying there and had celebrated my marriage within its walls. Of course, I'd done my best to bury those memories as deeply as I could.

I fought against the comfort and peace exuded by the place as I followed my elder up the stairs, through the stark exterior door, and into the courtyard. Amongst the trees, shrubs, and potted flowers, four divans were arranged around a long wooden table. On it sat a variety of ceramic dishes containing olives, cheeses, and fruits, and a platter of some sort of redolent meat—lamb, I gathered. Clearly, the spread had been prepared recently: the fragrant meat still sizzled. I could feel myself salivating and realized that I had no idea when I had last eaten or drunk.

As my former teacher reclined on the divan nearest three olive trees, the setting sun cast a rosy glow on his snow-white hair. "Eat," he prompted, "please, my son."

When I merely sat there, mute and stupefied, he rose and approached me, his knees protesting as he crouched by my side. Very gently, he speared two morsels of lamb and held them out to me.

He would serve me?

My appetite overcame my self-loathing, and I accepted

his offering. In moments, I was greedily devouring the delicious morsels and reaching for more. Nothing had ever tasted so good.

Gamaliel returned to his divan and quietly watched as I enjoyed the repast. When I leaned back, finally satiated, he said, "Saul, you will sleep here. Sarah has the guest room ready. She has also drawn a bath, which I suggest you make use of now." At that, he smiled—for the first time since he'd accosted me at the Assembly.

Finding no words with which to thank him, I rose, swayed, and recovered myself—but not fast enough to escape my mentor's scrutiny. Placing a hand on the back of the divan, I nodded my reassurance that I was well, and hoped my sincere gratitude was also conveyed at that moment.

Sarah appeared as if summoned and motioned me to follow her up the stairs to the roof for my bath. I followed her, but slowed when I heard Gamaliel call out, "Saul …."

I turned to find him standing at the bottom of the stairway, shielding his gaze from the setting sun. "Yes, Rabban," I answered.

"You must stay away from the Temple for the next several days. Rest here, and regain your strength. I insist upon it."

"Yes … thank you, Rabban … for everything." Suddenly, I could barely summon the energy to climb the rest of the stairs, let alone disagree with Gamaliel's directive.

Sarah's slim form had changed little in the ten years of my absence, and the dark hair that flowed down her back remained mostly free of gray. *She is still a beautiful woman,* I mused, *though probably in her late sixties.* I wondered where Simeon and his sister Ruth were living now.

I lurched back to the present as Sarah pointed to the bath and smiled. "Take your time, Saul," she said softly.

XXXIII

Looking around the lovely sun-filled bedchamber at the rose curtains and colorfully decorative urns and tables, I could almost persuade myself that I was at our old home in Tarsus. *Sarah's decorative sense is remarkably similar to my Hannah's,* I thought, smiling. It's no wonder that Hannah had loved Sarah from the moment they met in preparation for our wedding.

I waited for my thoughts to plunge me into despair and was surprised when that did not happen. In fact, the memories of my dear departed wife inspired twinges of joy, along with gratitude for the years we had shared.

I took a few moments to orient myself. I felt rested, but what time was it? The sun was low in the western sky. I knew I had bathed the previous evening but must have slept until late afternoon.

Taking my time dressing, I considered the kindness and generosity of Gamaliel and Sarah and wondered how I could possibly repay them. These musings were interrupted by a soft knock.

"Saul, are you awake?" The voice belonged to someone younger than Gamaliel. *Could it possibly be ....*

I opened the door and was immediately enveloped in a bear hug. "Simeon!" I breathed, as he intoned "Saul!" into my long, curly hair. Pressed tightly against his lean chest, with his heart beating against my own, I closed my eyes in pleasure and wondrous memory. Simeon had been the brother of my heart since my earliest school days.

"Father sent me up to make sure you were all right," he said, stepping back to examine me. "You've been asleep for over two days!"

"But Simeon," I said, perplexed, "that cannot be. I bathed in the upper courtyard just last evening!"

Simeon's startling green eyes, so like his mother's, crinkled in amusement. "Saul, you came up here to bed several nights ago and have been sleeping ever since. No matter. Mother has prepared lamb and lentil stew and her special almond honey bread to celebrate your return to Jerusalem. My mouth has been watering for hours, but she'll not serve any of us until you are sitting at the table. So I am begging you—get dressed! We all need to eat!"

The meal was indeed magnificent. Sarah, resplendent in a violet linen tunic cinched in gold, bustled about, happily serving her men. A filmy veil floated over her dark hair, secured to the crown of her head by an ivory pin. Not for the first time, I thought she must resemble her biblical namesake, Abraham's own wife. Catching me looking at her as she served her son a third helping of stew, she asked, "Saul, is the meal not to your liking? Are you not feeling well?"

I realized that having no interest in eating, I had been toying with the delicious food in front of me. I looked down at the platter and—to my horror—saw it filled with blood. Although I knew this was a hallucination, another crazed image from my boiling mind, I pushed myself back quickly from the divan. Springing to my feet, I swayed, then crashed to the floor.

XXXIV

⌒⌒⌒

"You gave my Sarah a terrible fright, Saul," said Gamaliel. "And the rest of us as well. I am so glad to find you better."

After my collapse at the table, I had once again slept through two cycles of day and night. I was finally beginning to feel normal ... or as close to that state as I could imagine. The evening breeze stirred up the subtle fragrance of the olive trees and that of an astounding variety of lovely pink, violet, and yellow flowering plants. Sarah's artistry in the garden was unsurpassed. Reveling in the peace and beauty of this place and the kindness and generosity of my hosts, I was flooded with gratitude. "Rabban, your kindheartedness is beyond description," I said. "I have not felt this well since before ...."

My explosive bout of coughing was initially meant to deflect the flood of memories that washed over me, but I found myself collapsing in genuine gasps when I inhaled some wine during the performance. Simeon jumped up from his divan and hurried to my side to pound me on the back. Recovering and nodding my thanks, I leaned back to catch my breath.

Father and son exchanged a look laden with—*what?* Foreknowledge, it seemed. I watched as Gamaliel nodded to Simeon, who cleared his throat, then did so again.

Why is he suddenly nervous? I wondered. *What could the only son of the most learned man in Judea be apprehensive about in my presence? This is the man who will take Gamaliel's place in the School of Hillel within the next decade, if not sooner....*

"Saul," Simeon said, dispelling my thoughts, "the divide between the Sadducees and us is widening. More and more of these so-called *Christians* are exerting influence over our people." He stopped and glanced at his father, anxiously.

Gamaliel's steady, hazel gaze never left the face of his son. "Tell him," he insisted quietly.

Simeon nodded and continued. "Two days ago, one of the leaders of the sect, a man named Peter, went to a house in Bethlehem in which a child had died. The mother had begged him to come, having heard about various miracles that had supposedly occurred in the name of the dead prophet, Jesus. Could Peter attempt to revive her only daughter, a child of twelve?

"Although it was a half-day's walk, he undertook the journey, and many followed. There was a crowd assembled outside the house when the child emerged onto the porch and waved. You can imagine the uproar! And now the mother is telling everyone that, through Jesus, this man Peter can raise the dead."

I sat mesmerized, hanging on Simeon's every word. When he'd finished speaking, my friend stared at me, but I do not think he saw me. I believe he was looking directly into the gaping abyss that was his future.

During the years I had studied at the Temple, I had observed the alternate rancor and forced tolerance with which the Sadducees and the Hillite Pharisees regarded each other. None of us students could have missed the philosophic and political differences rending the two groups. Rigidly conservative, the Sadducees derived from the priestly, aristocratic class of Jews while the Pharisees were primarily merchants like my father and his. The Sadducees made up the majority of the Sanhedrin Council and scoffed at the notion of eternal life, angelic beings, and resurrection. Following the political ambitions of their forefathers, they answered to Annas and his son-in-law, Caiaphas, who had held the Chief Rabbi position for decades.

We Pharisees, by contrast, represented the common people and were championed by them.

Like his grandfather, Hillel, Gamaliel's views were those of the scholar—measured, balanced, and thoughtful. He was every inch a Hillel Pharisee and the very antithesis of the rigid, domineering attitudes of Caiaphas.

"Caiaphas wants these leaders jailed," explained Simeon, his eyes darting about the courtyard nervously, "and possibly even tried for treason. He insists that they are guilty of blaspheming the Lord."

Why does this make you so afraid, my good friend? I wondered silently.

"Simeon fears more violence," Gamaliel explained as if reading my mind.

XXXV

Simeon and I sat in the uppermost row of the Sanhedrin Council. Although only an apprentice, Simeon had been told to take the seat next to mine, reserved for the newest member of the Council.

Eight rows down, in the first row, sat Gamaliel, two seats away from Annas and Caiaphas. It had been more than a week since I had been there and, although I was far more alert and rested than I'd been at my last session, the cacophony in the resonant Chamber of Hewn Stone was making it impossible for me to think clearly, or to understand what any one individual was shouting.

Caiaphas had opened the meeting with another tale of the new zealots, this one about a man known to most of Jerusalem as a frequent beggar at the Beautiful Gate. The previous afternoon, according to the High Priest, Peter, the disciple, had caused trouble with his bizarre response to the beggar's plea for alms.

When members of the Council demanded details, Caiaphas nodded and left the chamber momentarily, returning with a man and a woman! Before the shocked Council members could protest this affront to tradition, the Chief Priest addressed them once more. "My colleagues," he began, "I am well aware of our prohibition of the presence here of any but Council members, as well as the traditional separation of women and men in any sacred gathering. Indeed, we have never before heard the voice of a woman in these meetings." He waited for a moment before continuing, adroitly building the tension among the seventy members. "But these are strange times, are they not? Times that demand flexibility and risk." Bowing to his colleagues, he introduced the two strangers as husband and wife, then turned to the man and said, "Please, tell them what you told me earlier."

The man's voice quavered as he recounted the miracle he had witnessed. "The man called Peter fastened his eyes upon the paralytic beggar," he said, "and then looked over at his friend, whom he referred to as John. 'Look on us,' he commanded the abject soul before them. Obeying his entreaty, the paralytic looked up at the two men, his hands outstretched in the expectation of alms. But Peter said, "Silver and gold have I none; but such as I have, give I thee: In the name of Jesus Christ of Nazareth, rise up and walk.' At that, Peter took the beggar by the right hand and lifted him up, and, as he did so, the poor man gained strength in his limbs. Soon he could stand on his own, then walk! He entered the Temple with his two benefactors, walking and leaping and praising God. Everyone assembled saw it with their own eyes—ourselves and at least fifty others. All were filled with wonder and amazement at that which had happened to a beggar well known to us."

The silence in the Chamber was absolute. Caiaphas stood mutely by the man for a moment, and just as the Council members began to recover their voices, he escorted the couple out of the Chamber.

When he returned alone, it was to an uproar of indecipherable voices that continued for some five hours.

XXXVI

"Arrest Peter!" someone shouted. "Crucify him and his helper, John!" cried another elder. In a flash, the entire Chamber galvanized into one voice, chanting, "Crucify them!"

We had been in session for almost eight hours at that point, and tempers were fraying. Voices were growing raspy. But finally, it seemed, the widespread sentiment had coalesced into this two-word call to arms. *Crucify them.*

Simeon and I exchanged a look as Gamaliel rose and glided across the narrow strip of mosaic tile separating Caiaphas and the Council members, then stopped and turned to face the gathering. Caiaphas was clad in his priestly vestment, and the contrast between it and Gamaliel's simple white tunic was glaring.

Even from our distance of more than fifty meters, we could see that Caiaphas had not expected this. Rigidly, he turned to his right and bowed to Gamaliel. I knew better than to hazard another glance at Simeon.

Although Gamaliel never made a move to silence the crowd or try to be heard above the melee, the Chamber grew as silent as it had been when listening to the stranger's testimony hours earlier. Very quietly, Gamaliel began to speak. To a man, each member of the council leaned forward in his seat to better hear the soft voice of the Rabban.

"Men of Israel," he began, "consider carefully what you are about to do to these men. Some time ago, the rebel Theudas rose up, claiming to be somebody, and about four hundred men joined him. He was killed, his followers dispersed, and it all came to nothing. After him, in the days of the census, Judas the Galilean appeared and drew people to his cause. He, too, perished and his followers scattered to the winds. So, when it comes to this present case, I advise you: Leave these men alone. Let them go! If their purpose is of human origin, it will fail. And if it truly is from God, you will not be able to stop them no matter what you do. You may even find yourselves fighting against God Himself."

Gamaliel bowed to the stunned assembly, then to Caiaphas, and returned to his seat. In the aftermath of his speech, it felt as if the very air had been sucked from the room, which grew oppressive, heavy, and sweltering in spite of the cool evening air.

With a nod to Gamaliel, Caiaphas said, "Men of Israel, we have heard words of wisdom. Let us heed them and disband for the next two days. I ask that each of you pray and fast, that we may receive the Lord's direction."

XXVII

The days and weeks dragged on. Although Gamaliel treated me as another son and Simeon could not have been more of a brother, I could not help questioning my purpose. Here I was, twenty-eight-years old, living in the home of my former teacher, eating the food cooked by his wife, earning none of my keep. Having regained my health, I felt like an athlete running in place ... warming up for a race that might never happen.

Council meetings had become predictable. Two or three times each week, another of Peter's miracles was reported, sparking conflict among the Sanhedrin. Respect for Gamaliel was such that no one—not even Caiaphas—was willing to oppose him, at least openly. Small groups of two or three members could frequently be seen conversing with the High Priest, but the conclusion reached during each open meeting was that Gamaliel's "wait-and-see" approach would continue.

Until news came of Stephen.

"Stephen was seen with Peter and some of the other Christ-followers walking through the Beautiful Gate this morning," Gamaliel commented casually one morning, as he sliced a fig in half and placed it on his plate.

Simeon and I looked at each other, aghast. *OUR Stephen, from the Temple? With those zealots?*

The close friendship of Stephen, Simeon, and I had been

an unlikely one, granted. Not only was Stephen older than the two of us by four years, but he was also from Galilee, where speech, dress, and religious customs are different from our own. While Simeon and I were descendants of the twelve tribes, Stephen's ancestry was a motley assortment of Aramaean, Iturean, Phoenician, and Greek. And yet, there was never a division among us, never a sense of superiority on anyone's part, never the case of two against one, and—perhaps most surprising—never any sense of rivalry. In fact, our differences sometimes helped us prevail. Stephen's more impromptu method of prayer was fortuitous on more than a few occasions.

I thought about the time we were given a rare afternoon off and decided to make good use of by exploring the area around Jerusalem. Simeon and I were about fifteen at the time and Stephen close to twenty—which made him the de facto ring leader.

Stephen had traveled more than we had and was more familiar with adjacent cities—including Bethlehem. I'd studied the place but knew only that it had once been called Ephrathah and that Jacob had buried his wife Rachel there. The notion of climbing through the Judean mountains and into such an ancient and storied town was irresistible to Simeon and me.

We took the northwestern road, which turned southwest to Bethlehem, calculating that it would take us about two hours to reach our destination. This would afford us plenty of time to explore it and return to Jerusalem before dark.

What we hadn't counted on was the goatherder.

I chuckled aloud at my memory of that day, attracting the attention of both Simeon and Gamaliel, who looked at me quizzically. In response, I said, "Simeon, do you remember the time Stephen led us to Bethlehem—and … we encountered that goatherder?"

Simeon's eyes widened, and he darted a look at his

father while suppressing laughter.

Gamaliel, who had methodically been slicing his fig into smaller and smaller bits, looked up from his handiwork and said, "Ah … the infamous journey to Bethlehem. Am I finally to get the truth about what happened that afternoon? Or should I say, that afternoon that stretched on through an entire night and most of the following day?"

Simeon and I looked down at the table, knowing there would be no escape.

Glancing toward the doorway where his wife had appeared and stood listening, Gamaliel smiled and said, "Sarah, come and join us. We have waited a long time to hear of this adventure." Turning back toward me, his eyes twinkling, he said, "Saul, please proceed. We eagerly await the tale."

XXXVIII

As we huffed our way up the steep mountain road, a bit of scripture came into my head and I couldn't help reciting it aloud:

> And as for me, when I came from Padan, Rachel died by me in the land of Canaan in the way, when yet [there was] but a little way to come unto Ephrathah: and I buried her there in the way of Ephrath; the same is Bethlehem.

"Oh, there goes, Saul," chided Stephen," our great scholar! Even when we have a precious few hours off, he quotes from the Book of Kings!"

"Stephen!" I responded, tapping him playfully on the shoulder. "That wasn't from the Nevi'im, for the Lord's sake! It's from the Torah, remember? Genesis, chapter forty-eight, verse seven, to be exact. We studied it just a few months ago!" I shook my head as if scolding him for his obtuseness but couldn't help laughing at the same time.

Stephen was right about me, of course—I was a scholar at heart and loved studying with Gamaliel. The fact that I could quote the Tanakh with ease almost compensated for my short stature and strange, bowed legs.

By contrast, Stephen was tall, like my father and Shimon. And even Simeon—whom I'd once been able to regard eye to eye—had grown several centimeters of late. My hope of growing into my name, which was a tribute to the imposing and robust first king of Israel, had waned with each birthday. I couldn't help feeling that my diminutive stature must be a disappointment to my father and the entire tribe of Benjamin.

The odd external rotation of my legs had been apparent from the time I'd first begun to walk. Although my mother thought it charming, she'd consulted a doctor who told her it was the result of some type of mineral deficiency that had stunted the growth of the bones in my lower legs. As I grew taller, the external cant of my limbs increased to the point that running in races or competing in the games became impossible.

Summoning what inner strength I had at that age, I decided that my intellectual gifts would simply have to eclipse my physical limitations. As you might imagine, that decision was not without cost. Most of the boys I encountered at school took an instant dislike to me. Thankfully, Stephen and Simeon seemed deaf to the derision of our classmates—a fact more precious to me now than it was at the time.

We were climbing the western side of the road, a challenging ascent that necessitated a lull in our conversation when suddenly, we found ourselves surrounded by an enormous herd of goats. Where there had been companionable silence, there was now a frenzied chorus of dogs barking, goats bleating, and distant shouts from a goatherder.

Simeon and Stephen began to drop back, clearly unnerved by the noise, which put them near a group of kids and their mothers.

No! I thought, my instincts as a flock-tender coming to the fore, *don't go near those kids! The dogs and goatherder will think you are—*

Before I could open my mouth to warn my friends, the four dogs tightened into a pack and commenced stalking Stephen and Simeon, who did the worst thing they could under the circumstances: they ran. Their flight carried them further into the herd, scattering the kids from their mothers. As I stood riveted, incapable of intervening, Simeon dropped to the ground with a yelp of pain and lay crumpled and unmoving.

Just then, the goatherder appeared over the crest of the hill, slingshot loaded with another considerable stone. Without hesitation, Stephen sprinted in a straight line toward the goatherder, scattering the herd and confusing the four dogs who parted with frenzied barking to let him through. As he approached the goatherder, he dropped to his knees, put both hands together as if in prayer, and shouted what sounded like a garbled mix of Aramaic, Hebrew, and another language I could not understand.

The memory of the sight was comical, for Stephen's running was graceless. Lanky arms and legs blurred, making him look like a bizarrely tumbling stick figure. That, coupled with the exhortation-like prayer at the feet of the astonished goatherder, sent both Simeon and me into gales of laughter as we recalled the incident—but our frivolity dried up instantly upon hearing Sarah say, softly, "Oh my son, you came so close to death." As I blinked my way out of the past, I watched as she sank down beside her son, her face exceedingly pale.

This was not a good idea, Saul, foolish of you to think it an amusing tale worth telling.

Gamaliel patted his wife's arm consolingly and looked intently at me. "What do you think prompted Stephen to do such a thing, Saul?" he asked. Before I could reply that I had no idea, Rabban forced a smile and urged me to continue. I wondered for a moment at his sudden interest in Stephen, then returned to the past.

Very slowly, I took a few steps toward the wary Idumean goatherder who stood as if paralyzed above the still jabbering Stephen. I extended both arms, palms stretched out and up in a gesture meant to signify, *Shalom ... we mean no harm.* I stopped about ten meters from the man and watched while he pocketed the slingshot and extended his hand to Stephen and helped him stand up.

For a few moments, we three stood regarding one another.

Pointing over at the still unmoving Simeon, the man's thoughts were evident in the expression on his dark, weather-beaten face even before he began shouting. Although I was unfamiliar with the nuances of his language, I gathered he said something to the effect of, "You should not be in this place! The injuries of your friend are his own fault—not mine!"

Somehow, his dark, terrified eyes and stooped shoulders brought to mind my old mentor, Eli. I remained still, and my silence seemed to calm him. Stephen murmured something in a language he seemed to understand, and he finally allowed his shoulders to droop. "I hope your friend is not badly hurt," he mumbled in rough Aramaic.

Anxious about Simeon, who continued to lay on the ground, too still and too pale for my comfort, Stephen and I crouched beside our fallen friend.

"That gash looks deep," I murmured.

With a contrite nod, the goatherder handed us a skin filled with water and motioned for us to use it to cleanse Simeon's bleeding forehead. When he saw we had no cloth to do so, he reached into one of many pouches within his robes and pulled out a clean, soft-looking cloth.

I soaked the cloth with the water, then held it gently against my comrade's forehead—at which point he sat up as if hit again. He raised his own hand to his head, then pulled it away when he felt the cloth.

"My head! What ... happened?" he cried, then fell back again in a faint.

"So *that* is how you got that scar, son," Sarah said as she trailed her long fingers along the rough and red raised skin on her son's forehead. Her color had returned, as had her usual cheery countenance.

Simeon grasped his mother's fingers and kissed them. "Yes, Mother. And, since neither Stephen nor I was in good enough shape to travel that night, we accepted the invitation of the herder to stay with his family." He looked over at me and smiled. "As I recall, Saul, you spent most of that night playing with those baby goats."

Smiling back, I said, "Not exactly playing, my friend. It took Stephen and me over six hours to help that poor herder gather up all the kids and new mothers! It was the least we could do, we figured."

Gamaliel regarded us all thoughtfully but said nothing more. I wondered why he had been so curious about Stephen's stunt. After all, he had shown the same impetuously dramatic flair when we'd acted out the Book of Job.

XXXIX

❦

"This Peter and his associate, John … did I hear someone say they were Galileans, Rabban?"

"Yes, I believe they are, Saul. Their accents are strongly northern."

Surprised, I said, "So you have gone to hear them speak?"

"Father and I have both listened to them," Simeon interjected as he toyed with his food, his demeanor now somber. "To be specific, they are from Betsaida."

I stared at him, then glanced at Gamaliel, waiting for some explanation. *What would have prompted these wise men to waste time listening to another in the endlessly long line of zealots?*

As quiet settled over the table, Sarah rose and returned to the kitchen with our mostly empty plates. Finding himself with nothing to tinker with, Simeon simply sat pensively, looking somewhere above my head.

Gamaliel regarded me but said nothing.

"That explains why Stephen would know them then," I remarked inanely, to fill the unbearable silence. "He married right around the time that Hannah and I did … and I believe they returned to Galilee afterward."

I expected no response and got none.

"Rabban," I persisted, hungering for the satisfaction of

my curiosity, "do you believe these so-called prophets to be imposters ... or ... something else?" Before he could answer, I declared with vehemence, "Peter claims to raise people from the dead! They must be fakers. Either that or ... in league with the diabolic!"

It was Simeon who replied. "Saul, the fact is, Peter takes great care to explain that he is doing nothing. That he *can* do nothing. He insists that all power resides in this risen Christ and that he is just a vessel—as we all are. All of creation, he declares— each one of us and all our surroundings—emanate from this God-man."

Without thinking, I murmured David's song:

For who in the skies above can compare with the Lord? Who is like the Lord among the heavenly beings?

In the council of the holy ones God is greatly feared; he is more awesome than all who surround him.

Who is like you, Lord God Almighty? You, Lord, are mighty, and your faithfulness surrounds you.

You rule over the surging sea; when its waves mount up, you still them.

You crushed Rahab like one of the slain; with your strong arm you scattered your enemies.

The heavens are yours, and yours also the earth; you founded the world and all that is in it.

You created the north and the south; Tabor and Hermon sing for joy at your name.

Your arm is endowed with power; your hand is strong, your right hand exalted.

Righteousness and justice are the foundation of your throne; love and faithfulness go before you.

Blessed are those who have learned to acclaim you, who walk in the light of your presence, Lord.

XL

AURELIUS

Mamertine Prison, Rome

I watched, somewhat surprised when Paul took my suggestion for a quick break. He strode about the tiny confines of the exquisitely small space where he had lived out the last eighteen months of his life. *Strode* is a bit of an exaggeration; his bowed legs and red, swollen knees looked painful as he moved.

Even silent, as Paul was then, the fire in him was almost tangible, seeming to wrap itself about his person and grow in intensity as the night wore on. That there was pain in both legs was unmistakable; but, it seemed to serve as fuel in some mysterious way. I could almost see the waves of energy emanating from him as he paced the perimeter of his cell.

I had lived just one-third of his years, but could not imagine being able to recall and recount my entire life story coherently. To do so while being held captive and facing death was unfathomable.

There were no windows in this fetid place, but I guessed the time to be two or three in the morning. I shuddered as I thought about the few hours of life this man had left and the genuinely terrible death that awaited him. I did believe in Christ, I told myself, *I did*—wholeheartedly. But … the qualifier, always the qualifier … was my faith as ironclad as his? Would I be able to face death with the equanimity that Paul seemed to? Especially if my death sentence were a direct result of my belief in a god other than Caesar?

Nero, a god! Such asinine absurdity.

As if reading my mind, Paul stopped moving. He regarded me curiously. "Why the grave countenance, Aurelius? What are you thinking about?" Before I could respond, he grimaced—finally revealing his pain—and said, "Do not contemplate my end, Aurelius—not yet, son. I am still breathing, and we have much more to do. Let us finish the task."

XLI

SAUL

Jerusalem

"You look exactly the same," I said—and he did. Although now in his third decade, Stephen was as lean as he'd been the last time we'd seen each other. If anything, he looked younger. There was a peace about his countenance, a sort of radiance flowing out of him. I knew that, like me, he had lost his wife and two children—not in an earthquake but from a deadly disease that had somehow spared him. The coincidence was eerie.

After Simeon and Gamaliel had told me they'd seen our old friend with Peter and his fellow travelers, I decided to look for him. I'd found being in the Jerusalem Temple and sitting with the Sanhedrin at once intoxicating and frustrating. On the one hand, the chance to associate with that distinguished group of lawmakers was beyond anything I'd dreamed of; on the other, the sense that I was simply running in place persisted. I couldn't help feeling that something colossal was germinating and that I was relegated to the sidelines.

Why did I feel so compelled to find Stephen?

I could think of a variety of reasons. Indeed, nostalgia for our boyhood friendship was one of them; so was pure curiosity about what Stephen had become. What had possessed my old friend to make him believe that the Messiah had been born a man, had died on a cross between two thieves, and—most absurdly of all—had risen from the dead?

In the three months since his crucifixion, I had listened carefully to all the tales being whispered about the life and death of this man Jesus. While the stories varied, the basics were always the same: Jesus had been born to an unmarried woman named Mary in Bethlehem—the very same humble village where Simeon, Stephen, and I had spent a night in the tent of a goatherder all those years ago. This was yet another curious coincidence, one that hovered in my mind. Many months into her pregnancy, a carpenter named Joseph had married her and taken her into his home. Shortly after the birth, a few of the elders whispered about the parents taking the child and fleeing into Egypt to escape King Herod's slaughter of all firstborn Jewish sons. I knew that such an execrable thing had actually happened, though it was before I was born. The supposed reasons for Herod's act ranged from insanity to the fear that a rival king—this Jesus—had been born in Bethlehem. According to the whispered gossip, the king had been alerted to this powerful presence by three "wise men" who'd followed a bright star to find the child.

That our own King David had also been born in Bethlehem added to the long string of the peculiar coincidences surrounding this man called Jesus and me.

Snippets of all these tales and more were colliding in my mind as I watched Stephen across the crowded marketplace, attempting to rekindle the exceptional warmth I'd felt toward him when we were young boys. Although he stood quite still, it seemed as if he were in motion ... rising upward, somehow. Catching myself before I called out, "Stay still, Stephen!" I stepped aside to avoid the jostling of a group of men hurrying toward one of the moneylenders. "My friend," I said, raising my voice over the commotion, "can we go somewhere to speak privately?"

We stood in the Court of the Gentiles, amidst throngs of people bustling about the various vendors selling animals for the annual sacrifices. Above the sound of pilgrims haggling loudly with money lenders, I thought I heard Stephen say something, but couldn't be sure.

Just then, a woman appeared with a young girl in her arms. I had not seen her approach, nor could I hear her cries, but her expression—a combination of desperation and determination— was enough to prompt people to make way for her. I could not imagine where she was headed because she would not be allowed past the Court of Women, and yet her gaze was focused upward. As she got closer, I could see that the child was stone still. Lifeless.

"Help me, please!" she cried as she passed to my left. "My daughter has been having fits for three days. Now she has collapsed, and I fear for her life!"

Incapable of looking away, I followed her slow progress with her burden. Ahead of her, I saw a man climbing up the stairway amidst the cloisters on his way to Solomon's Porch. As I watched, he lifted his tunic to ascend the stairs, revealing stocky, hairy legs. Although the bedlam must have made it difficult to hear her high-pitched voice, he stopped and turned around, as did several men accompanying him. They were all dressed in the same simple, colorless tunics and robes.

The man changed course and began to descend toward the woman. As he did so, I thought, *He looks like me—ten, maybe fifteen years older, but we could be brothers.* He was short in stature, with a large nose and scraggly beard sprinkled with white. His legs were bowed, though nowhere near as much so as my own. All things considered, he was quite unattractive. Like me.

Somehow, I knew I was beholding the man called Peter. Despite his ordinary dress and unprepossessing demeanor, there was something about him—some energy or force—that demanded attention.

As Peter neared the woman, he said something, but too softly for me to hear. Then he took the child from her arms, clasped her to his own breast, raised his eyes to heaven, and said something else—again inaudible to me. After a moment, the child stirred in his arms and began to cry. Was this a miracle happening before my eyes? In confusion, I turned to Stephen for his response to the event but saw only strangers.

Stephen had disappeared.

XLII

‿‿‿‿‿

It had been a week since I had seen Stephen and his new associates. I had said nothing of my experience at the Court of the Gentiles to either Simeon or Gamaliel. Although I had no desire to keep secrets, I knew that if I spoke of my encounter with Stephen—if you can call it that—then I would have to explain why I went looking for him. I couldn't do that, because I didn't know. Even after seven days, I continued to be puzzled by my own motives. *What had drawn me to seek out men whom I considered enemies of the faith? And what did the seeming "resurrection" of that dead child mean? Had it been the result of some kind of magic? Sorcery? Could I even trust my own eyes?*

So, I said nothing, and neither of my hosts noticed my silence because they were absorbed in Council matters. It seemed that Stephen had become loquacious over the past week, and a number of our synagogues were growing agitated over his remarks. This did not surprise me because, having witnessed him with my own eyes, I understood that the Stephen I had known—the carefree and imperturbable young man—was gone. In his place was another man, someone alien to me.

Caiaphas and Annas were once again in charge. The anxiety galvanized by the behavior of Peter and his associates had restored their authority over the Sanhedrin. I was only marginally familiar with the Libertines, Alexandrians, and Cyrenians, but knew them to be from a Hellenized synagogue. I recalled that Stephen had been born in Greece; his family had moved to Galilee when he was a small boy. Therefore, unlike many Galileans, Stephen spoke Greek fluently, albeit with an amalgam of accents.

As I sat in the council chamber listening to Caiaphas relate the latest of the complaints against Stephen, I considered the strange dynamic at play. It seemed we were less inclined to be forgiving, more willing to believe the worst of those with whom we were most familiar.

"They are accusing him of blasphemy! Saying that he has performed demonic deeds such as causing the paralytic to walk, the dead to live, and numerous other evil actions."

I sat wondering about this. Peter was the one who had empowered the paralytic to walk, and it was he who had brought the seemingly dead child to life. Stephen had merely stood watching, as had I.

But I said nothing.

From the back of the room came a shout: "Bring Stephen here!"

Immediately, a chorus of voices joined in the exhortation. "Let the Council decide!" they cried. "We must determine what these men are up to!"

Most of the seventy assembled men rose to their feet, while Simeon and I, seated in our usual spots near the back wall, looked at each other in wonder.

XLIII

When Caiaphas finished the long list of charges against Stephen, he asked him, "Is this true? Did you say and do these things?"

Undaunted by the charges, his command appearance before the Sanhedrin, or the knowledge that he faced certain death, Stephen answered unhesitatingly, and at extraordinary length. "Brothers and fathers, listen to me! The God of glory appeared to our father Abraham while he was still in Mesopotamia. 'Leave your country and your people,' God said, 'and go to the land I will show you.' So Abraham left the land of the Chaldeans and settled in Harran. After the death of his father, God then sent him here—to the place where you are now living—without any inheritance or land of his own. Although Abraham was childless at the time, God promised him that he and his descendants would possess this land. 'For four hundred years, your descendants will be strangers in a country not their own,' proclaimed the Almighty, 'and they will be enslaved and mistreated. But I will punish the nation they serve as slaves, and afterward, they will come out of that country and worship me in this place.' Then he gave Abraham the covenant of circumcision and Abraham became the father of Isaac. Isaac became the father of Jacob, and Jacob became the father of the twelve patriarchs.

"Because the patriarchs were jealous of Joseph, they sold him as a slave into Egypt. But God was with him and rescued him from all his troubles. He gave Joseph wisdom and enabled him to gain the goodwill of Pharaoh, king of Egypt. So Pharaoh made him ruler over Egypt and all his palace.

"Then a famine struck all Egypt and Canaan, bringing great suffering, and our ancestors could not find food. When Jacob heard that there was grain in Egypt, he sent our forefathers on their first visit.

"On their second visit, Joseph told his brothers who he was, and Pharaoh learned about Joseph's family. After this, Joseph sent for his father Jacob and his whole family, seventy-five in all. Jacob went down to Egypt, and that is where he and our ancestors died. Their bodies were brought back to Shechem and placed in the tomb that Abraham had bought from the sons of Hamor at Shechem.

"As the time drew near for God to fulfill his promise to Abraham, the number of our people in Egypt had greatly increased. That is when a new king, to whom Joseph meant nothing, came to power in Egypt. He dealt treacherously with our people and oppressed our ancestors by forcing them to throw out their newborn babies so that they would die.

"At that time, Moses was born, and he was no ordinary child. For three months he was cared for by his family. When they hid him outside for his own safety, Pharaoh's daughter came upon him and brought him up as her own son. Moses was educated in all the wisdom of the Egyptians and grew powerful in speech and action.

"When Moses was forty years old, he decided to visit his own people, the Israelites. He saw one of them being mistreated by an Egyptian, so he went to the man's defense and killed his Egyptian oppressor. Moses thought his people would realize that God was using him to rescue them, but they did not.

"The next day, Moses came upon two Israelites fighting. He tried to reconcile them by saying, 'Men, you are brothers;

why do you want to hurt each other?' But one of them pushed Moses aside and said, 'Who made you ruler and judge over us? Are you thinking of killing me as you killed the Egyptian yesterday?' This prompted Moses to flee to Midian, where he settled as a foreigner and had two sons.

"After forty years had passed, in the desert near Mount Sinai, an angel appeared to Moses in the flames of a bush that burned without being consumed. Amazed, Moses approached to get a closer look and heard a heavenly voice say, 'I am the God of your fathers, the God of Abraham, Isaac, and Jacob.' Moses trembled with fear and did not dare to look. 'Take off your sandals,' the Lord said, 'for the place where you are standing is holy ground. I have indeed seen the oppression of my people in Egypt. I have heard their groaning and have come down to set them free. Now come, I will send you back to Egypt.'

"This is the same Moses who had been rejected by one of his own with the words, 'Who made you ruler and judge?' He was returning at the bidding of God himself, as their deliverer. After acting as the conduit for many miracles, he led his people out of Egypt to spend forty years in the wilderness. This is the Moses who told the Israelites, 'God will raise up for you a prophet like me from your own people.'

"But our ancestors refused to obey him. Instead, they rejected him and, in their hearts, turned back to Egypt. While Moses was atop Mount Sinai, receiving God's commandments, they approached his brother Aaron and demanded, 'Make us gods who will go before us. As for Moses who led us out of Egypt—we don't know what has happened to him!'

"Our ancestors then made an idol in the form of a golden calf. They brought sacrifices to it and reveled in what their own hands had made. In anger, God turned away from them and gave them over to the worship of the sun, moon, and stars. This agrees with what is written in the Book of the Prophets: 'Did you bring me sacrifices and offerings forty years in the wilderness, people of Israel? You have taken up the tabernacle of Molek and the star of your god Rephan, the idols you made to worship. Therefore I will send you into exile beyond Babylon.'

"Our ancestors had the tabernacle of the covenant law with them in the wilderness. It had been made as God directed Moses, and our ancestors—under Joshua—carried it with them when they took the land from the nations God drove out before them. It remained in the land until the time of David, who enjoyed God's favor and asked that he might provide a dwelling place for the God of Jacob. But it was Solomon who built a house for him. However, the Most High does not live in houses made by human hands. As the prophet says: 'Heaven is my throne, and the earth is my footstool. What kind of house will you build for me? Or where will my resting place be? Has not my hand made all these things?'"

As the members of the Sanhedrin sat mesmerized by his oration of a story they knew well but were somehow hearing anew, Stephen pointed an accusatory finger first at one side of the room, then the other. "You stiff-necked people! Your hearts and ears are still uncircumcised. You are just like your ancestors in the desert: You steadfastly resist the Holy Spirit! Was there ever a prophet your ancestors did not persecute? They killed even those who predicted the coming of the Righteous One. And now you have betrayed and murdered him. You have received the law that was given through angels but have not obeyed it!"

And then he quieted, his face shining so brightly that it was as if a lamp had been kindled within him. That sense of upward motion I had perceived in my old friend a week earlier was absent. The man I saw now bore no resemblance to the one I had known since childhood. This person was the personification of peace, wholly unmoved by the danger he was in.

As their shock at Stephen's remarkable soliloquy wore off, various Council members began to shout, "Blasphemy!" "Seize this man!" "Outrageous!"

Stephen continued to stand motionless at the front of the Chamber as if they were applauding his oration. His only response, as the threats rained down around him, was a slight, respectful bow of his head.

I dared not glance at Simeon, for I trusted he thought as I did—that our old friend Stephen, who had not been able to retain even the fundamental teachings of the Torah when a student, had just delivered an eloquent history of the Chosen People. And he had finished by accusing all of us of killing the Righteous One.

XLIV

Caiaphas demanded that each Council member stand and offer his verbal assent to Stephen's sentence for blasphemy: death by stoning. Annas began by standing and uttering a forceful "yes." Jacob tood up next and assented without hesitation to the execution of one of our own. A few, like Eliezar, spent five or even ten minutes opining about the righteousness of the killing. I welcomed the time-consuming digressions because I had no idea what I would say when my turn came. I could claim that I must abstain due to my longtime personal relationship with the condemned, as Gamaliel had done and as I expected Simeon to do.

But there was an argument taking shape in my mind, and I could not quiet it.

Just who is Stephen to appear before this eminent assembly and pronounce us "stiff-necked?" Who is he to fling the words of Moses like stones against his elders? Who is this Greek-speaking Galilean who has suddenly and mysteriously attained the oratorical skills of Cicero? And finally, how is it that Stephen condemns the entire Sanhedrin for murdering a mere pretender? He is breaking the twenty-sixth law: the command to love all human beings in the covenant. Or does Stephen now contend that the covenant has changed? That is indeed blasphemy.

In this room sit scholars of priestly families that date back centuries, including members of my own tribe of Benjamin, the "least of the tribes." Yes, there are conflicts among this diverse group of Hillel Pharisees, Sadducees, Freedmen, Essenes, Alexandrians, Cyrenes, and countless other Hebrew sects, but they are minor in the face of this betrayal. This son of Israel has committed the most unpardonable of sins. We are brothers, chosen by God, and Stephen has broken both the Mosaic and the covenant made with Abraham. Insisting that Gentiles, the uncircumcised, are included in the covenant, is just one of many heresies. Stephen must die.

My relief at coming to this dire conclusion was akin to sexual release; purpose and meaning had found me, and my sense of aimlessness was dispelled. I understood what I was to do—my mission. At that moment, I knew why the Lord had taken my family. Like Joshua and King David, I would lead the tribes of Israel against these hypocrites, liars, and deceivers. It was what I was born to do. This time, no one—not even Rabban Gamaliel—would stop me from fulfilling my lifework.

I did not hear Simeon's vote to abstain when he stood to cast it.

Ignoring a voice that whispered, *Do NOT do this thing!* I jumped up and barked out my "Yes!"

A few minutes later, we all filed out to the courtyard where Stephen stood waiting, a serene expression still suffusing his face. I stood in the back, far away from the enormous piles of stones that sat silently waiting to collide with flesh.

The rocks began to fly toward Stephen. As one after another connected with his face and head, he started to bleed. I thought back to our mishap with the goatherder, whose correctly aimed shot had felled Simeon instantly on the road to Bethlehem. Unlike him, Stephen stood firm for more than ten minutes, absorbing an impossible hail of rocks. Finally, one of the elders cried out, "Blasphemer," picked up the most massive stone he could lift, and hurled it at the back of Stephen's knees. Stephen dropped to the ground, and the air grew thick with the sickening sounds of rocks pulverizing flesh.

It will be over soon.

But suddenly, improbably, Stephen sat up, pointed at the sky, and cried out, "Look! I see heaven opening and the Son of Man standing at the right hand of God. Lord Jesus, receive my spirit."

My childhood friend's last words were, "Lord, do not hold this sin against them."

Without giving the battered, broken body another thought, I strode over to Annas and Caiaphas, who stood quietly talking by the Chamber of the Nazarites.

"You need a warrior to lead the fight against these heretics," I declared.

Startled, Caiaphas peered at me as if trying to place me.

"My name is Saul of Tarsus, sir. I studied here under Rabban Gamaliel for six years. I have returned to Jerusalem because I lost my family and business in the Cilician earthquake and now sit as a junior member of the Council. I am the man you have been looking for."

Knowing that I had their attention, I quoted the prophet: *Be amazed at this, O heavens, and shudder with sheer horror, says the Lord. Two evils have my people done: they have forsaken me, the source of living waters, they have dug themselves cisterns, that hold no water. I had planted you, a choice vine of fully tested stock; how could you turn out obnoxious to me, a spurious vine? Though you scout it with soap and use much lye, the stain of your guilt is still before me, says the Lord God.*

Caiaphas started to speak, but his father-in-law Annas laid a suppressing hand on his arm and, in a reed-thin voice, said, "Saul of Tarsus, your heart is on fire with the spirit of the Lord God of Israel. It is clear that you have been sent to save Jerusalem." Straightening out his arm and extending his fingers, he said more forcefully, "Bow your head for my blessing, young man." These words could plainly be heard at the other side of the courtyard, where Gamaliel, Simeon, Nicodemus, and the rest of the Hillel Pharisees stood.

Startled but pleased at the former High Priest's attention, I bowed my head obediently.

Annas placed his hand on my head and prayed:
Hear, O Israel: The Lord is our God; the Lord is one.

And you shall love the Lord, your God, with all your heart and with all your soul, and with all your means.

And these words, which I command you this day, shall be upon your heart.

> *And you shall teach them to your sons and speak of them when you sit in your house, and when you walk on the way, and when you lie down and when you rise up ….*

The crafty old priest was offering the evening Shema! With my head still bowed, I could see from the corner of my eye the space around us filling up with Council members who had scattered in an attempt to distance themselves from the gruesome spectacle in which they'd participated. Evening prayers were obligatory.

XLV

Sarah intuited the tension emanating from her men when we returned from the Temple. Once she had quietly served us all, she left without a word to go about her other duties.

I was ravenous and ate as if I had not seen food for a week. To my right, Simeon reclined and ate nothing, merely sipped his wine. Gamaliel had taken tiny portions, which he pushed about on his plate and only occasionally nibbled at.

"Saul, you are my good friend," said Simeon, "but I must tell you how disappointed I am in your decision to side with Caiaphas and the Sadducees against Father and me."

I looked over at him, stung by his reaction. "Is that how you see it, Simeon? That I *sided with* the others against you?"

Refusing to meet my eyes, he nodded, then examined the beautiful mosaic tile of the courtyard as if seeing it for the very first time.

I sat motionless, working hard to suppress my furious reaction. My teeth ground together as I closed my eyes and recalled my years of study with Pylenor. *This is his opinion, Saul. Only an opinion. Simeon has every right to believe the action you took was purely political.*

The thought calmed me, and I relaxed my rigid, defensive posture. *From Simeon's viewpoint, I can see why he believes that I have changed my loyalties. After all, Gamaliel has been generous with his hospitality. For nearly three months, I have accepted his food, lodging and—*

Gamaliel interrupted my thoughts. "Saul, Simeon does not speak for me," he said, stretching out an arresting upraised palm toward his son, who had half risen to his feet in objection. Turning to Simeon, he said, "Son, I know all too well how heartbroken you feel about what happened today. My heart is heavy, too. We have lost a beautiful soul in Stephen. We all witnessed the light that poured out of him as he testified." My teacher turned his calm, kind, gaze toward me as if applying a balm but continued speaking to his son. "I know Saul saw it as well."

"Yes, Rabban, I saw the light … and heard his words … but—"

Gamaliel raised his palm once more, but this time in my direction. "I know you, Saul of Tarsus—perhaps better than any living person in this world." He smiled the saddest smile I had ever seen. "One of the great gifts of advanced years in this faith of ours is the acceptance of mystery, blindness, and chaos as part of God's plan." His voice dropped then so that I was forced to sit up and lean forward to hear what more he had to say. "Should we accept only good from God and not accept evil?"

The tears that had stood dormant behind my eyes were freed by his quote of Job's rhetorical question and rolled down my face. My mind flew to the time when we'd studied with this great man. We'd spent nine months on the Book of Job, culminating in Stephen, Simeon, and me being recognized as "Job scholars."

"I have no idea what God wants of you, Saul. None. But I have no doubt that you are being used by Him." He looked kindly over at this son, whose gaze was still cast downward. "Simeon, there is nothing shameful in defending your father. But in making such a hasty judgment about your friend, you have made a mistake. It may seem reasonable to you to assume that Saul's 'war against the Christians' is undertaken for his own political gain. But sometimes we are called upon to be far more than reasonable. Now … I hope you will apologize to our guest."

XLVI

Awakening from a profound sleep, I found myself momentarily disoriented. I was encased in the dark. Groping about, I touched and peered through heavy curtains. Nothing looked familiar. My sleepy gaze traversed the vastness of a bedroom fit for a magistrate or high official. The large bed I lay in was as soft as a cloud. They'd enclosed me in the absolute darkness, which accounted for the depth of my slumber.

An ornate marble table sat at each side of the bed, atop a particularly decorative mosaic floor that featured geometric and floral patterns within concentric square bands. At each corner of the room stood a column that climbed gracefully to the ceiling, embraced by elaborate circular designs of gold and ivory.

This is a room for kings and emperors, not a goatherder-turned-warrior from Tarsus. My smile was grim as I recalled just where I was and why.

I was living in the Antonia Fortress. I knew, as did any observant Jew, that Herod the Great had built the place, which stood within the angle formed by the northern and western colonnades of the Temple, and had named it for his friend Mark Antony. Antonia Fortress dominated the Temple, its central tower, and four turrets rising hundreds of meters into the sky. It was clad in polished stone to prevent anyone from scaling it.

Caiaphas had contacted Gamaliel and suggested I move

there since I would be working closely with the Sanhedrin while I put together the band of men to do battle with Jesus' followers. Although we'd all smiled at one another respectfully when I had left Gamaliel's, I suspected that even Sarah was relieved to see me go.

When finally, I roused myself and drew back the bed curtains fully, I was horrified to see the height of the sun. I dressed quickly and hurried down the stairs and through the Nicator Gate, then up through the cloisters to meet with Caiaphas and his advisors.

"Forgive me, I—"

Cutting me off with a wave of his hand, the High Priest said, "Sit, Saul. Please sit."

A servant approached with a tray of hot tea, warm slices of bread, and yogurt. I nodded, and he placed it on a small wooden table beside my chair. Caiaphas was engaged with a few men I had not met, which gave a bit of time to drink the tea and eat a few morsels.

The quarters were spartan compared to my own: a few simple chairs, benches, and divans surrounding the periphery of the room. The only sign of Caiaphas's status was the height of his high-backed chair; he was not wearing the robes of his office, but instead a plain gray tunic, neutral-colored shawl, and matching turban.

Idly, I wondered who the men were he was talking to and decided they must constitute the leadership of the Temple Guard. If so, they were the men with whom I would work.

Caiaphas led them to where I sat, and I stood to meet them. "Saul, may I introduce Shimon, Eli, and Davide." We all nodded awkwardly as Caiaphas briefly described their backgrounds. My heart hammered in my chest because I was entering a world I understood little of. These were men of the street, or they looked as if they were. Shimon was about my height but stockier than I; he looked as if he could lift a full-grown bull without breathing heavily. Eli was his opposite: tall, wiry, with just a small beard at the tip of his chin. These two regarded me with little interest, but Davide broke away from them and offered a deep bow. "Saul of Tarsus, I have heard of you, sir, and look forward to ..." He hesitated.

Abruptly, I was assaulted by doubts, second thoughts, and uncertainty. *What on earth could we name this thing we were about to do? Where has all that passion and fire gone, Saul of Tarsus?* Willfully, I stomped on my sudden fear, stepped forward to meet Davide, and bowed back to him. "The *cleansing,*" I said. "I believe that is the word you are looking for. We are cleansing our Chosen People of the pretenders, heretics, and blasphemers, Davide." I glimpsed Caiaphas nodding vigorously a few feet away. His dense beard covered most of his face so that his expression was hard to read, but the approval in his eyes was evident.

XLVII

"Saul, we need to know where these followers of the dead prophet are hiding."

I nodded at Davide but said nothing, just cast a quick glance over at his two comrades, who stood pretending not to listen.

Following my eyes, Davide waved off to the two men, who moved toward the fountain beyond a patch of olive trees—far enough away that we two could speak in private. Looking back at me, he continued, "I grew up in the Lower City and know most of the old Hebrew families there. I will take you down to meet some of them. During the conversation, they will naturally tell you how sorry they are to hear about the loss of your family and business." Davide scrutinized me as he spoke, and I guessed his thoughts. *Is it wise to talk so candidly to this stranger? Will he accept the counsel of a mere guard?*

Caiaphas had earlier given me a brief history of Davide, Shimon, and Eli. The latter two were Assyrian and had been servants before being promoted to Temple Guards. Davide was entirely different. As far as I knew, he was the son of a poor Hebrew family, and yet he had somehow gained the wisdom—or was it simple cunning—of a learned man. He had advanced to the rank of Captain and conducted himself with confidence and ease.

Nodding, as if I had spoken my thoughts aloud, Davide said, "We guards are invisible to the priests. Aside from Rabban Gamaliel and a few others, we do not exist. In the course of my duties, I have listened in on many secret meetings carried on by Caiaphas, Annas, and the Elders. These grew especially heated during the fearful days when Jesus returned to the city. These men were frightened of Pilate—almost as much as of Jesus. They seemed to be concerned that he might not do as they wished: crucify Jesus.

"Rabbi ..." He shifted uncomfortably. "Saul ... may I speak frankly?" At my nod, Davide continued, "you should know that I was the guard who carried the false evidence against Pilate created by Caiaphas and Annas, accusing him of stealing Temple funds to build the aqueduct to Rome."

False evidence of stealing? Caiaphas manipulating the fates of great men? I knew him to be ambitious and crafty, but this? Did Gamaliel know about it ... approve of it?

Davide's mouth formed a smile, but his eyes remained dark. If anything, there was an implied challenge in his expression, "When I hesitated, not knowing how to refer to the actions we are embarking on, you said to call it a *cleansing*. An apt description but understand this: Those willing to purge must be willing to plunge deeply into filth."

Just who is this man who speaks to me so familiarly? Who baits and challenges me?

Staring into Davide's dark-brown gaze, I tamped down my rage and willed my wounded pride to ebb away. *He is merely explaining why and how he can help ... even lead. This faked information he refers to, involving a dead Roman prelate I did not even know ... this does not concern me. During the days when those actions were taken, I was living happily with Hannah and our boy, oblivious to what was coming our way.*

"You have my undivided attention, sir," I said quietly.

Go on."

"Once I have introduced you into the homes of my people, and you have allowed them the courtesy of offering their consolation, the talk will lead to our current mission. We will be able to elicit from them the information we require to get our job done. They will know which families have become heretics. I promise you, my mother and others will have knowledge of each one of them.

XLIII

Davide and I walked quickly along the narrow dirt street of the Lower City, passing small, tightly packed rows of limestone houses stained an ugly yellow-brown from years of wind and sun. The difference between this place and the Upper City, with its blinding white palaces and villas, was astounding. My mind churned with what had happened over the two days we'd been walking these hot, dusty streets.

My partner, for that was indeed the only term for Davide, had proved himself invaluable; his knowledge of these people's customs was vast. We had just completed our last and thirtieth visit to a local family—a lengthy stay, as these were Davide's parents and two sisters. Until my meeting with Davide's mother, I had remained untouched by the attempts at consolation for my losses. But the tall, slender elegance of this woman, Esther, brought to mind my oldest sister—her namesake—so profoundly that I was forced to step outside to collect myself.

Upon my reentry, Esther mercifully asked no more questions of me, nor did she attempt to offer any words of sympathy. It became clear to me that she was the source of Davide's quick intelligence and tact, as well as his firmness of personality.

Exhibiting utmost graciousness, Esther insisted that we partake of a small supper with her and Davide's young sisters. Her husband, she explained, was working in the field they shared with four other families.

Her dimpled smile was irresistible, as were the tantalizing aromas wafting from her fireplace. I could not refuse this charming woman; I soon found myself sitting at a simple table on the hard-packed dirt floor of the small home, surrounded by Davide's family. Although the room was utterly without adornment, the fireplace, beds, lamps, and other simple furnishings were neat and clean. Through a door at the back of the room that led to an enclosed yard, I could hear the gentle mewing sounds of a lamb or two, an ass, a cow, and a few chickens.

Esther poured a drop of wine into my cup, then waited patiently for me to try it. "Is it to your taste?" she asked, her brown eyes crinkling at the corners.

One sip explained her suppressed smile. She must have known how excellent her family vintage was. "Esther, this is the best I have tasted since leaving Tarsus," I said, smiling, secretly surprised at how comfortable I felt around this woman and her family—far more so than in the spectacular surroundings of the Antonia Fortress.

As much as I was enjoying the repast and company, the lowering sun beckoned. "Davide, we must reach the Temple before sunset," I said, receiving a nod in return.

The information we had collected was invaluable. As Davide had predicted, the members of this cult of Jesus were well known to their neighbors: some thirty families had joined Peter and his group. Included in our intelligence were facts about the heretics' children and other family members.

After about thirty minutes of hasty travel, we arrived at the Temple, where we were to meet with the entire body of the Sanhedrin and answer any questions about the planned removal of the heretics from the city.

Their concerns were reasonable.

"Now that they have been identified, what will be done to these people?"

"Will they be stoned? Banished from Jerusalem?"

"What about their young children? After all, we want no duplication of Herod's slaughter of infants three decades ago."

Nicodemus, a Hillel Pharisee for whom I had great respect, had asked the questions about the fate of the Christ-followers' children. A wise and learned man, he'd accepted my explanation of how we'd identified the heretics. I'd outlined our talks with the local people, and the way neighbors had revealed the secrets of neighbors. It was clear, he pointed out, that these people we sought believed their dead prophet worth dying for. Few of them, if any, were likely to deny their affiliation with the sect.

Nicodemus's logic quieted some of the older Council members, who seemed incapable of listening to me, but his persistent queries about the fate of the children gave me an idea. "I thank you for your comments, Rabbi Nicodemus," I said with a slight bow. "And it strikes me that the answer to your questions about the proper care of innocents has already been supplied by Rabbi Mordecai."

Nicodemus's normally placid countenance gave way as both eyebrows shot up in surprise. Rabbi Mordecai was in his late nineties and barely knew what day it was, but it had been he who had asked about banishment. His reedy, peevish questions—*Will our own people be banished from Jerusalem? Are we to create another Babylon?*—had annoyed most of the Council, especially since he had waited until almost the end of the fourth day to bring up the subject.

Nodding at Nicodemus, I looked up at where Mordecai sat and said, "Rabbi, your idea has great validity. Any heretics we encounter with large families can be escorted from the city with assurances that they will be welcomed back as soon as they renounce this pretend Messiah—this Christ—but not sooner. The rest will be flogged and then banished."

XLIX

ℭ━✦━☉

After stealing a few hours of sleep, Davide and I met with Eli, Shimon, and two more men whom Davide had told me about. I nodded when Davide introduced us but forgot both names instantly. My heart thundered in my chest, I was breathing fast and feeling more anxious than I had in my life.

Our states of mind are peculiar, are they not? For, quite clearly, I had been far more distressed during that desperate ride on horseback from Tarsus to our farm after the earthquake—but that harrowing episode was fast receding behind this new and alarming task I had volunteered for.

Thoughts of Gamaliel kept appearing in my head: of his silence during the previous evening's Council meeting; of his consistent kindness and generosity toward me, contingent on nothing. Not even loyalty. I had taken it all for granted. Had I been honestly grateful, or too consumed with thoughts of myself to respond as the man had deserved?

What kept niggling at me most was my former teacher's utter trust in God. What must it feel like to have faith like his? I kept hearing him say, in his quiet and reasoned voice, *Should we accept only good from God and not accept evil?* And, *I have no idea what God is doing with you, Saul. None. But I have no doubt that you are being used by our Lord.*

As I stood on that street corner, I became so absorbed in

questioning myself—second-guessing my actions—that I missed whatever it was Davide was trying to say to me. I was roused from my thoughts only when he reached out and gripped my shoulder and hissed, "Saul, this is *your* mission. Take control."

It was too late for second thoughts. I was committed.

"Forgive me, I— Davide, you ride with ..." I waved toward the two men whose names I had forgotten. "I'll ride with Eli and Shimon."

We had agreed to ride the horses supplied by the Sanhedrin to the Pool of Siloam, tie up our mounts there, and continue on into the Lower City on foot. Stealth was critical, though we figured it was inevitable that news of our presence would quickly circulate among the sect. Once that happened, any families with the ability to leave would probably attempt to do so.

It was three a.m. as we approached the house. I told Eli and Shimon to stand behind me, and after what felt like an eternity, I raised my fist. The sound of it against the door was explosive in the quiet of the moonless night.

The door opened immediately, and a man about my age stood before me, hair and beard askew. A woman and two small children hovered behind him.

"Is this the house of Ben Abram?"

"Yes. How can I help you?"

The politeness of the man seemed incongruous and threatened to uncloak my fake sense of bravado. Unnecessarily loudly, I said, "I am Saul of Tarsus. I have been elected by the Temple Sanhedrin to identify all heretics and blasphemers in Jerusalem. Are you a follower of Jesus—the one they are calling Christ?"

I had expected any reaction but the one I got. The man's wife stepped up beside him, holding a young child in her arms and pushing an older one before her—a son. "Yes, Saul of Tarsus," she interjected. "We have been baptized and are followers of Jesus." Her large, expressive eyes shone; there was no fear or defiance in them, nor in her simple declaration.

For a moment, I was dumbfounded at the serenity upon her face. It was the same look I had seen on the countenance of Gamaliel. For just a moment, I thought of Dienekes telling the remnant of the Spartan warriors who would die that day that the opposite of fear was not courage but love. That noblest of leaders went on to tell his bruised and battered men that the bravest of all warriors were the women. Staring into the eyes of this young wife and mother, I understood.

Tearing my gaze from her, I directed myself to Ben Abram. "You have twenty-four hours to leave Jerusalem. If my men or I find you in the city afterward, you will be stoned for blasphemy against the Lord of Abraham, Isaac, and Israel. Do you understand me?"

"I do," he said.

Four hours later, having visited more than twenty houses, we were back at the Pool of Siloam to retrieve our mounts and head back to the Upper City and the Temple. Only two of the homes we'd approached had been vacant; the rest had been occupied by families similar to that of Ben Abram. All but one family had accepted the ultimatum to vacate with equanimity, though none had been willing to renounce its affiliation with the false messiah.

The exception to this acquiescence came from a widow with a paralyzed daughter. Scoffing at the notion of evacuating—and as unwilling as the others to deny the dead prophet—she declared, "If we must be stoned, so be it. I am a widow, I have no son to support me, and my daughter cannot move. I can go nowhere, Saul of Tarsus. When you return in a day, I will be here because this is my home." As I walked away, shaking my head at her defiance, she had called out something so odd that I could not get it off my mind: "Saul of Tarsus, you cannot take my life, for I live in Jesus. He who has risen lives."

As I rode back to Antonia Fortress and my plush surroundings, I wondered just what I would do with this woman. What *could* I do?

L

⚬⚬⚬⚬⚬

"I am ready. And so is my daughter Ruth. Do you need to bind us?" She extended her arms toward me as she asked the question.

I peered into the dark confines of the single-room home and saw a girl of about seven lying against a wooden recliner, her legs thin and flaccid. She held out her hands as well.

This house was the last one to be checked. We'd found all the others vacant, their owners having exiled themselves from Jerusalem as they'd agreed to do. This was the house I'd dreaded approaching.

If she had not been so emaciated, this woman—named Abigahil ben Hur—would have been beautiful. Her eyes were a coppery brown and seemed huge on her face, which was sharply defined by high cheekbones and a strong jaw. How I had hoped that she would not open the door; that someone had taken pity on her and spirited her away. But, there she stood, staring at me, unafraid and … something else. Relieved?

I wondered how she and her daughter had come to be in such dire straits. Did not these people help one another? Could not Peter have healed this girl, as he had that infant at the Temple? Immediately, I rebuffed that thought. Something else had gone on that day—some kind of sorcery.

Impatient, Abigahil took a step toward me, arms still outstretched.

"Put down your arms, woman," I said harshly. "I am not going to bind you or your daughter."

My show of mercy to these people had clearly nonplussed Davide. Our original plan had been to gather them up and take them to the courtyard at the Temple, where they would be publicly flogged before banishment. But, the previous evening, when we had learned that all but one would leave Jerusalem, I'd decided to just let them go; I had no stomach for more bloodshed. There would be no public flogging of the blasphemers before they were banished.

Davide and several of the morbid onlookers he'd amassed had reacted with astonishment when they saw the empty courtyard. Those of the Sanhedrin merely shrugged and ambled off to their homes. To his credit, Davide had not questioned me about why I had changed my orders … which suited me well because I had no answer. My mind was churning. More accurately, it was boiling. While I had been thoroughly exhilarated at the discovery that my life had a purpose—that all that had transpired before, the intense studies, fervent love for family, and sacrifice had led to this moment—I doubted my persecution of these people. I wanted to deny Peter's supposed "miracle," but how could I disbelieve what I had seen? As I'd watched, he had raised his eyes to heaven, said some words, and the child before him had returned to life!

Although I yearned with all my will to justify my consent to Stephen's horrific execution, I could not. Echoing through my soul were the last words of this man who had been my friend: *Lord, do not hold this sin against them.* Nor could I deny the reality of the voice I had heard commanding me to vote against his stoning.

"Well?" Abigahil demanded, shifting from one foot to the other and holding my gaze with an expression that seemed like … was it pity?

"Woman!" I bellowed, "why are you hastening your own death and that of your daughter? All we ask is that you disavow your belief in this fake Messiah. Do that now, and I will leave you to live out your lives in peace!"

How could I do this thing? Send a woman and innocent child to their deaths? Why could she not simply deny the dead man who'd claimed to be a prophet?

Eyes luminous, Abigahil said almost tenderly, "Oh, Saul of Tarsus, Jesus is no fake Messiah. He is Life. Truth. The Way. There is no peace without him."

The way to what? I wanted to ask but caught myself before uttering the words. I recalled the story of Jeremiah, the prophet who had tried to run from Our Lord, claiming that he was too young to be the voice of God. I would need his steadfast faith to face the next hour of bloodshed. Next, the prophet David's words came into my mind.

His enemies whisper together against me.
They all weigh up the evil which is on me:
Some deadly thing has fastened upon him,
he will not rise again from where he lies.

I had recited that psalm throughout my boyhood. Never did I dream that I would become the "deadly thing fastened upon him," but no other description was as apt. I was personifying evil and knew no way out.

LI

Again, I had heard that voice.

Saul! Do not do this.

Again, I had ignored it.

I swallowed the bile crawling up my throat and turned away from the mangled, brutalized bodies of Abigahil and her daughter. As I scanned the crowd of onlookers, I fought an almost irresistible urge to smash away the smug, satisfied looks on many of the faces. The watchers had carefully stayed far enough away to avoid the bright-red spurts of blood that were now turning to black as they pooled and congealed between the cobblestones and across my tunic.

Finally, I saw him. Pushing my way through the crowd, I shouted,

Thus says the Lord:

What fault did your fathers find in me that they withdrew from me, went after empty idols, and became empty themselves?

They did not ask, "Where is the Lord who brought us up from the land of Egypt,

Who led us through the desert,

through a land of drought and darkness,

through a land which no one crosses,

where no man dwells?"

The crowd parted, their faces filled with apprehension and dread at the sight of me striding through the courtyard, blood-soaked and quoting the Book of Jeremiah at the top of my lungs. I am confident that I looked crazed. I *felt* crazed as I stomped over to Caiaphas to demand—not ask, "Give me letters of introduction to the churches in Damascus! Jerusalem is cleansed. Now, we will journey southeast to Damascus to locate and rid our Chosen People of the pretenders there."

Caiaphas nodded so vigorously that I thought the motion would tip him over. *He fears me,* I noted with surprise. The smile I allowed to play across my lips was cruel and bitter. I held the old man's gaze while intoning more of Jeremiah's words and watched his eyes widen, and his long beard jump with his repetitive swallows.

"Be amazed by this, O heavens,
and shudder with sheer horror," says the Lord.
"Two evils have my people done.
They have forsaken me, the source of living waters;
they have dug themselves cisterns,
broken cisterns that hold no water."

Then I switched to the Prophet Habakkuk:

"Are you not from eternity, O Lord,
my holy God, immortal?
O Lord, you have marked him for judgment,
O Rock, you have readied him for punishment!
Too pure are your eyes to look upon evil,
and the sight of misery you cannot endure.
Why then do you gaze on the faithless in silence
while the wicked man devours one more just than himself?
You have man like the fish of the sea,
like creeping things without a ruler."

These passages from my boyhood studies sprang to my lips effortlessly, heightening the ghostly, uncanny sense that enveloped us both as we stood facing each other. The Court of the Gentiles was now wholly empty as even the most ghoulish of the onlookers had fled my fearsome ranting. I felt possessed by these holy men of old; my eyes witnessed their visions of doom, destruction, and wrath from the Holy of Holies. My entire being felt on fire.

Caiaphas trembled. Alternately, his aged fingers grasped his ephod, breastplate, and girdle as if looking but not finding firm purchase. Finally, shakily, he said, "The letters. Yes, I will get them for you." When I did not respond, his voice rose in pitch. "But surely you can't mean ... *now*?" Coughing in an attempt to recover his dignity, he willed his voice back down to its normal range. "Saul, you want me to get you the letters to the Damascus churches right now? It is nearing midnight. Surely you do not intend to leave tonight!"

"Indeed I do, Caiaphas. I will wait here for your return."

LII

⟨⟨∘⟩⟩

Davide did not object when I hammered on the door to his quarters in the middle of the night, shouting, "Get up! We need to get on the road to Damascus NOW!"

In a matter of seconds, the door flew open, and there he stood, fully dressed. "I'll get the horses if you wait here, Saul. We will be there by evening prayers, I swear it."

"No need, my friend," I responded. "Caiaphas has already helped me fetch them from the stables. They are tied up outside."

I ignored the look of shock on his face and counted the men who had gathered behind Davide. "There are just six horses," I said, confused at the fact that there were now eight of us.

"Who are these two new men?"

"I decided we could use the assistance of Aaron and Samuel," David replied, "since Damascus boasts four large synagogues. They have been with the Guards for as long as I. We can trust them."

Davide watched me, clearly curious to see how I would respond. *Is he testing me? Does he wish he were in my place?* Quickly, I decided that his motive was pure—that he meant only to aid our efforts in any way he could.

"Fine then, I understand," I replied calmly. "Find a couple more horses and let us get started."

The road to Damascus was packed dirt with dangerous pits; it was not the kind of paved Roman road we were accustomed to. This made for slow going. Rather than the ten days I had hoped the journey would take us, we would be doing well if we reached the city by the end of the following month.

On the afternoon of the second day, as we began to climb the foothills of Samaria, Davide came abreast of me. "Saul," he said, "there is a spring fifty meters east of here, bordered by a grassy field. It would be an opportune place to water the horses and set up camp."

I nodded but didn't respond. I wanted to keep pushing and hoped Davide would understand the urgency without my stating what was evident.

"Saul. Even if you do not need sleep, the men and horses do." Davide spoke slowly, carefully, as if talking to a child or someone ill-versed in Aramaic.

Reluctantly, I nodded a second time, suddenly aware that I could not recall the last time I had slept. *Three days ago? More?* Having not ridden for such a long period since my journey from Tarsus, I was dreading the act of dismounting. It is incredible how quickly one's muscles can lose the rhythm necessary to establish harmony with his horse.

"Saul! Saul! Wake up!"

Blinking furiously, I shook my head in an attempt to determine my whereabouts. Davide was crouching next to me, brow furrowed, holding a cup of something steaming. Blinking furiously, I worked to pull myself away from the bloodied corpses of Stephen, Abagahil, and her daughter, whose name I had never bothered to learn.

"Can you sit up, Saul? This will help you recover your wits."

I took the cup and breathed in the steam that emanated from it. "What is this foul-smelling stuff?" I asked my cohort.

"It's tea made from some leaves my mother gave me when we visited her last week. She feared our mission would give me nightmares and insisted that this herb would relax and soothe."

Gingerly, I took a few sips of the scalding brew, figuring the pain might prove more salutary than the tea.

Davide then handed me a swath of folded fabric.

"What is this, then?"

"A new cloak and tunic. Go bathe in that stream over there, Saul. Your cloak is stiff with the blood of your victims. It even stains your face and beard. No wonder you were moaning in your sleep; this business would give anyone nightmares."

My head throbbed, and my body was racked with pain. Why I lay prostrate on the ground was still a mystery. Moving my head slowly and carefully, I attempted to get my bearings. The night sky was moonless and cloudless—a black void revealing nothing. *Why don't I hear the nickers of the horses or voices of the men?*

After four weeks of arduous travel, we were finally on the outskirts of Damascus. The last thing I recalled was telling Davide that we would reach the first of the synagogues in just a few more hours.

I sensed a presence beside me. "Who is there? Davide, is that you?"

"Yes, Saul. I am sitting right beside you, more relieved than you could ever imagine seeing you awake," he said, his voice reed-thin and quavering. It did not sound like Davide's vibrant, confident voice at all, but that of a far older man ... a petrified one at that.

"Why am I on the ground?" I asked, panic rising in my voice. "Did I fall off my horse? Why is there no campfire? And where are the others?"

Raising my hands to my face, I rubbed my eyes in an attempt to see him, but the darkness did not dissipate.

"I ... cannot explain what happened to you, Saul. It was a fearsome, terrifying thing. One moment, you were riding along at a cantor, clearly eager to reach our destination. Then, suddenly, the sky lit up brighter than a thousand suns ... a blazing, blinding light! Your horse reared up at the sound of a fearsome voice from the heavens, proclaiming, 'SAUL, SAUL, WHY DO YOU PERSECUTE ME?'

"At that moment, you fell from your horse." I heard Davide draw a shaky breath and then let it out very slowly. "This happened last evening, just after twilight. I have been sitting beside you since then, fearing that you were dying. I know of no better words to describe a thing that defies explanation, Saul—I apologize for that. But I have no doubt—" Davide's voice quavered and then lowered to a whisper, and he choked out, "that this was the voice of *God*." He was breathing rapidly now, almost panting. "When I raced over to you to see if you were all right, you were lying on your back, motionless. I shook you, hard and shouted at you, but you did not speak or move ... until now. You ask why there is no campfire, Saul. It is because it is midday. The sun is shining brightly. You cannot see it because your eyes are covered with a white, thick film ... somehow you have been blinded! And you hear no voices but mine because our men and horses have fled. Believe me when I tell you that my vigil of the past eighteen hours has been a terrifying one."

Blind?! I blinked rapidly, willing my eyes to adjust sufficiently that I might see Davide's face, but the impenetrable blackness remained. As the hammering in my head began to subside, my memory glimmered with the light Davide had described. And that voice ... that awful voice.

"Who are you, Lord?" I had asked, but I had known the answer before He'd spoken it.

"This is Jesus whom you are persecuting," he'd said.

I had heard that voice before. Suddenly, I was consumed by a terror like nothing I had ever experienced. The absolute darkness that met my open eyes was akin to the vast abyss of despair I felt in my mind and heart.

I tried to get up but fell back once again. My hands reached out, groped the darkness.

I was truly blind.

"Saul," said Davide, no doubt touched by my dread. "Here. Grab my hands."

When I found purchase, I steadied myself and rose with liberal help from my friend. "What are we to do?" I asked plaintively.

"We are going to do as the Voice directed and proceed to Damascus, where we are to be further instructed."

Feeling like a sightless, helpless baby, I hung onto Davide for dear life, incapable of placing one foot in front of another without his aid. I lost count of the times I fell, incapable of processing even his simplest instructions.

After what seemed like days of excruciatingly slow progress—but was probably just a few hours—I could hear people speaking, shouting, laughing. We were in Damascus at last. But I would be delivering no letters. Nor would I be persecuting any of the people of the Way.

Once again, I thought of Gamaliel's comments to Simeon on our last evening together: "One of the great gifts of advanced years in this faith of ours is the acceptance of mystery, blindness, and chaos as part of God's plan," he'd said. And then, "Should we accept only good from God and not accept evil?" After quoting Job, he had returned his attention to me. "I have no idea what God is doing with you, Saul. None. But I have no doubt that you are being used by Our Lord."

LIII

The Street Called Straight

"Why are you stopping, Davide?" My voice was shrill to my ears—like a woman's or like Caiaphas in the Court of the Gentiles. I stood trembling before the man I once considered my adversary.

Fear. All I knew now was dread: darkness, confusion, the abject horror of losing all that I had considered part of myself. Now, I am a pusillanimous, tottering shell of a man. In truth, I no longer have the right to be called man.

Since I could no longer rely on the sight of a stream, the stars, other men, the horses to calm me, I plunged ever more deeply into myself—my character and my flaws—than I had ever done.

For three days, my only cues as to the passage of time had come from Davide. My self-loathing was eclipsed only by clear, stark images, far more vivid than memory, of Stephen as friend, Stephen as apologist, and finally, Stephen as a bloody corpse.

Ever since my boyhood, I had felt the weight of my namesake Saul, the first King of Israel. I had always roiled under the futility of living up to the gigantic dimensions of this man; had been humiliated by my short, squat stature in contrast to King Saul's regal height, and the majesty of the priestly tribe of

Benjamin. But now, forced into introspection, I came to see Saul's disobedience to the Lord, his jealousy of David during the first battle with the Pharisees, his unremitting egoism, his vanity. The accusatory question of the Prophet Samuel rang in my ears—"What have you done?"—followed by Saul's weak excuse for his actions: "When I saw that the army was deserting me and you did not come on the appointed day ... so I thought I should sacrifice the burnt offerings."

Samuel's pitiless response to my namesake felt now as if it were directed toward me: "You have acted foolishly! Had you kept the command the Lord your God gave you, the Lord would establish your kingship in Israel forever; but now your kingship will not endure. The Lord has sought out a man after his own heart to appoint a ruler over his people because you did not observe the command the Lord gave you."

This was not the first time that I had pondered the strange conjunction of King David and me, Saul of Tarsus.

During the rare moments along our journey, when I summoned sufficient perspective to stand outside myself, the successive ironies of my life overwhelmed me. The loss of my entire family was merely a past sorrow when compared to the bottomless pit of my current condition. Like a helpless newborn, I could do nothing independently—feed myself, walk, or even evacuate my bowels. And never did the memory of that Voice, the one I had disobeyed not just once but two times, leave my psyche. I knew it to be the voice of Jesus. Was I to die and experience the fires of Gehenna?

Davide's voice penetrated my self-absorption. "Saul, there is a man named Judas who knows you by name. He has sent a servant to ask that we follow him to a street called Straight. That is where we stand now. The servant has gone into the house, and I expect the owner, this Judas, to appear momentarily. Once he does so, I will be on my way. I must return to Jerusalem,

Saul. I have been gone for far longer than I had planned."

Was he to leave me with this stranger? It seemed impossible that the abject terror I had felt since my sudden blindness could amplify, but it did. A few remaining shreds of dignity prevented me from dissolving into sobs and begging Davide not to leave me. My quavering response to his departure brought to mind Caiaphas at the Court of Gentiles. Had I felt even a drop of sympathy or pity for the fear I was inducing in him? Although I wanted to believe that I had felt compassion, the truth was, I had felt nothing. Caiaphas had merely been an instrument to me—a way to procure the documents I needed to embark on my campaign of intimidation, persecution, even murder if necessary.

Had I enjoyed the killing? Had the stoning of Abagahil and her daughter been pleasurable for me?

No. Not pleasurable. I had not been able to stand back from this bloody deed as I had done with the stoning of Stephen—not if I wanted to preserve my credibility with the Sanhedrin, Davide, and the Guards. But ... why had I found and thrown the most substantial stones of all? Had it been necessary to stand so close to my victims that their blood drenched my cloak and tunic?

I had behaved in this way to prove—to myself, first and foremost—that I was not a coward. I had shown weakness the week before, in letting so many heretics leave the city unscathed. I couldn't deny what I knew in my heart: that I had bludgeoned those two women to death to prove that I was a courageous soldier for the Lord of Abraham, Isaac, and Jacob.

But, in doing so, I had shown myself to be the most craven of all.

Job's heartfelt prayer that he'd never been born came to my mind, and I recited it with my entire being.

What a waste of muscle and sinew and brain and energy I was! My heart filled with gratitude that none of my family was alive to see the depths of depravity to which their son, husband, and father had plummeted.

LIV

Damascus

I was kneeling in prayer in the courtyard of Judas's house when I heard someone approaching. His voice sounded like that of an ancient man—quavering, timorous, hesitant—like someone approaching eighty years old.

"Who is there? Is that you, Judas?" Although I knew it could not be the young owner of this house, anxiety propelled the words.

"Brother Saul, I am Ananias. The Lord Jesus, who appeared to you on the road as you were coming here, has sent me so that you may see again and be filled with the Holy Spirit."

He approached and laid his hands on me, making me shrink back and begin to tremble. My hypocrisy knew no bounds. Here I was, begging for death, but the moment I sensed a possible threat, the pusillanimous Saul returned.

I could hear the surprise in his voice as he said, gently, "My son. There is nothing to fear from me, nothing at all. Try to relax."

At first, his hands felt warm, then like hot coals on my shoulders. He uttered some words in Aramaic so softly that I could not understand them, then shouted, "SAUL! Open your eyes and SEE!"

I jumped at his thunderous speech, then did as he commanded. To my great astonishment, I could see! Light, forms, colors, details—everything. Why had I never taken the time to give thanks for such a gift? I made no attempt to wipe away the tears rolling down my cheeks.

Squarely in front of me, I encountered the face of a gentle man ... his soft white beard, his lined cheeks, his kind and penetrating eyes. "Sir ... Ananias, how can I thank you? How did—" It was all I could do to keep myself from embracing and kissing him.

"My friend, it is not me you should thank," he interjected. "It is the spirit of Jesus. I am a mere instrument in his service." The chubby, bearded face split into a wide grin, and the eyes twinkled. "You, Saul of Tarsus ... our Lord has great plans for. Starting now."

Blinking away my tears, I repeated stupidly, "Great plans ... for what?"

"Saul, we are journeying to Ephesus. The Lord has directed me to take you to meet two people there. Our carriage awaits, so come—we have a long way to travel."

I hesitated ... still dumbfounded at the turn of my circumstances.

"Do you fear *me*, my son? Why, Saul of Tarsus, it is nothing compared to my own fear in coming here. All of Damascus has heard of your threats and the stoning of His people. The Lord Himself had to persuade me to journey to the home of Judas! I have seldom been so afraid as when I turned onto the street of Straight. The entire way to this place, I talked to Jesus: 'Lord,' I said, 'if this is the way you will me to leave this earthly existence, so be it.' Over and over, I told myself to be brave, but my terror could not be quelled."

"You were afraid ... of me?" I queried him. "Surely, you felt my tremors under your hands when you placed them on me ... the way I shrank at your touch like a timid mouse."

The man's portly belly shook with laughter. "Saul of Tarsus, destroyer of the church in Tarsus ... a timid mouse?! Come! We have no time to waste."

We had been traveling for close to a week, and Ananias had outdone himself in hospitality. He was evidently a very wealthy man, and his carriage was opulent. Instead of the hard plank benches of most such conveyances, his were lined with thick cushions. The openings in the walls of the sizable coach were extraordinarily generous, allowing the sunshine and air to pour through as we traveled. Ananias's two servants were experienced horsemen and commanded the four Friesian horses with skill and dexterity. In all, the journey was the most relaxing and comfortable of my life. Our inland route had been expertly paved by Roman soldiers, so the motion of the carriage was a gentle rocking from side to side, akin to the movement of a cradle.

Thus, the days passed in a hypnotic blur. On rare occasions, I tried eliciting details from Ananias on the subject of my regained sight or the reason for our journey. He simply smiled in a way I can only describe as paternal and said, "Saul, there will be time enough for all of that later. Now, you must concentrate on healing your mind and heart."

This had the effect of returning me to my semi-somnolent state.

Ananias had instructed the men to stop for the night in Samasota, a prosperous Syrian city at the mouth of the Euphrates. While the servants combed down, fed, and watered the horses, we walked past the vast barns of hay toward an inn.

Until we entered the vast building, which was crammed with long wooden tables surrounded by Roman soldiers, farmers, and merchants, I had not felt hungry. But, the rich aroma of the food made me suddenly ravenous—more so than I had been in recent memory. I smiled at the sensation, aware that it was a sign of returning health.

At each inn we encountered, Ananias enjoyed instructing me in the local cuisines and entertaining me with his stories. The fare for this evening was lentils and chickpeas, green salad, and a local fish I had never heard of but thoroughly enjoyed.

As generous as Ananias was with his time and tutelage, there were questions he would not—or could not—answer. Each time I asked why we were traveling to Ephesus, or with whom the Lord had commanded that I meet, he evaded the question. It happened so often that I finally asked, "Why, Ananias, why won't you explain the purpose of this journey?"

He responded without a glimmer of his usual good humor. "It is not my story to tell, my son," he said gravely. "It is the Lord's."

LV

AURELIUS

Mamertine Prison, Rome

I interrupt Paul's story at this juncture because none of his followers has ever read the details of those last days when he was known throughout Judah as the Jew who destroyed the Jerusalem Church. Those who had heard the tales of the murderous young Saul of Tarsus discounted the stories as either hyperbole, jealousy, or slander against Paul. For those of you reading this, these tales are undoubtedly long gone, lost in the mists of time. You might be tempted to believe that the Paul who traveled throughout the Roman Empire for over thirty years, enduring shipwrecks, floggings, imprisonment, and banishment, is the man born Saul of Tarsus; that the name change to Paul was merely a concession to Rome ... a device to become more acceptable to the Gentiles of the time. Thus, you may overlook the reality that Paul was a new creation. Saul's extraordinary conversion at the hand of Jesus served as both death and rebirth. The person known as Saul of Tarsus died during that fall from his horse and subsequent three days of blindness, and the new man, *Paul,* was born.

When Paul wrote these words in his letter to the Corinthians, he did so from his own experiences, about which you will read in the remainder of this missive.

So, whoever is in Christ is a new creation: the old things have passed away; behold, new things have come. And all this is from God, who has reconciled us to himself through Christ ....

Paul's words are poetic, lyrical—so much so that we are tempted to put them to song, as we do with the psalms of David. Perhaps this suggests that his tale is an allegory, but we must not let ourselves be misled. We who live in Christ have also been reborn into a brand new entity.

Need I tell you how I agonized upon hearing and having to record Paul's constant and unremitting self-flagellation during those last weeks before his conversion? At that point, we were very close to the end of his final letter, and Paul and I both sensed that dawn was approaching.

More than once, I suggested he rest from the ordeal of revisiting these terrible memories ... that surely he exaggerated his feelings and actions in the telling. I begged him to consider shortening or even deleting the stoning of Abighail and her daughter. "What purpose does their story serve?" I asked. "How would knowing about your murderous past help any of us? The events you speak of took place more than three decades ago—years before most of your followers—including me—were born."

"NO, Aurelius!" he insisted. "Write this *precisely* as I say it! All must know who I was, what I did, what I was capable of. Only then can they understand the *immensity* of the gift we receive! Only then will they comprehend that the words you write tonight—and all of the thousands of words I have written over the last decades—are not mine. How could they be? How could such a contemptible man write of such truth, wisdom, beauty, mercy, forgiveness?"

Only that once did this saint raise his voice to me. During the endless weeks when I'd treated him so ill, he'd been nothing but pacific, meek, and kind. His ire was aroused only when I attempted to mitigate his self-condemnation.

The second reason I interrupt is to explain the last two scrolls of Paul's final letter: the words you are about to read. These happenings in Ephesus will strain your credulity, for they are decidedly uncharacteristic of the man you've come to know. What you are about to read is pure mystery, consisting of the visions given Saul by the two people whom Christ loved best: His mother and His beloved disciple, John. I assure you, these words are strictly Paul's own. That you understand precisely how our esteemed Paul was able to write all those letters— to the Hebrews, Philippians, Romans, Ephesians, and Colossians— was of dire importance to him. Lest any consider that they derive from any source but the Spirit, he reveals where he journeyed during the months that followed his sudden blindness and the miraculous restoration of his physical and spiritual sight.

LVI

SAUL

Ephesus

Only tangentially was I aware that Ananias was leaving. The woman standing in front of me, before a stone hearth, so gladdened me that I was barely aware of my surroundings. It was not just that she was handsome—for beautiful was far too common a word to describe her—but that there was a radiance streaming from her very essence. The air about her veiled head shimmered. And her eyes ... how could I find words to describe a gaze of such purity and innocence? Without even thinking, I fell to my knees.

"You are His mother," I sighed.

Although she had not uttered a word, her gaze plunged deeply into my soul, causing a tearing sensation that I believed must be my heart bursting from my chest. But when I looked down, I saw no wound, merely the light-brown woolen cloak Davide had given me. As I knelt on the brick hearth, I believed I would die from this pain, and yet, I *wanted* it ... *needed* it.

Unaccountably, I became aware that the woman before me was being used by her Son in some mysterious manner. *This is cleansing, Saul. This unbearable pain is lustration, atonement.* I shrank from the word—the very one I had so foolishly bran-

219

dished before Davide and the Sanhedrin in my benighted attempt to do the work of the Lord. *Cleansing.*

I do not know how long I knelt on that hearth. It could have been hours or even days, but the last words I heard while on my brutalized knees were these:

> *Your name is no longer Saul. You are Paul now, Apostle to the Gentiles. The uncircumcised. You no longer live but have died. It is I who live in you, Paul.*

The words I heard next flattened me. I was being told the story of human salvation from the lips of the God-man whose followers I had pledged to destroy. How could I, a wrecked speck of humanity, warrant an explanation of how and why the Lord came to this earth? And yet, He continued speaking to me:

> *I who, although I was in the form of God, did not deem equality with God to be grasped at.*
> *Rather, I emptied myself, taking the form of a slave.*
> *Being born in the likeness of man, I was known to be of human estate.*
> *Obediently, I accepted death—even death on a cross!*
> *And it was thus that I humbled myself.*
> *Because of this, God highly exalted me,*
> *bestowing on me the name above every other name.*
> *For, at the name of Jesus, every knee shall bend,*
> *in heaven, on earth, and under the earth.*
> *And every tongue shall proclaim,*
> *'To the Glory of God, Jesus Christ is Lord.'*

"Paul, my brother, I am John."

I opened my eyes and blinked several times. The sound of a human voice was startling after hearing only the inner voice of Jesus. *How long had I been immersed in his voice? How long? If my knees were to offer a clue, I'd say I'd been on them for many hours.*

I did not ask how the man before me knew to call me by that name. I knew only that the place I found myself was like no other on earth. The stone floor, brick hearth, the very air seemed suffused with wisdom not accessible since the Garden.

He extended his right hand, which held a small piece of bread, and said, "The Lord Jesus, on the night he was betrayed, took bread, and when he had given thanks, he broke it and said, 'This is my body, which is for you; do this in remembrance of me.'"

I looked at him uncomprehending, and he held my gaze. His hand moved closer to my mouth, and he nodded once. I opened my mouth and took the morsel in. He smiled slightly, then reached up to the mantle behind him and took down a chalice. He extended it to me, saying, "This cup is the new covenant in my blood. Take this, and whenever you drink it, let it be in remembrance of me. Whenever you eat this bread and drink from this cup, you are proclaiming that the Lord died for you."

I took the cup and drained it dry. John closed his eyes and bowed his head and I did the same, aware that the agonizing pain in my knees had vanished. Unbidden came the words of the Lord to Moses in the desert:

> *Behold, I will bring down manna from heaven which has been reserved for you from the beginning. When the children of Israel saw it, they asked, "What is it?" And Moses said to them, "It is the bread that was reserved for you from the beginning in the heavens on high; and now the Lord is giving it to you to eat." This was the Bread of the Presence. The Bread that Moses, Aaron, and the seventy elders ate when they ate and drank with God.*

My breath caught, and my heart fluttered as I recalled the words of the prophet Baruch. As if a veil had been lifted, I saw Simeon, Stephen, and myself—Gamaliel's three top students—during the week before we left the Temple. Gamaliel had offered us a few days of study in the Zohar, the text of the Kabbalists. It was a rare offer, and we had gladly accepted it.

And it will happen that when all that which shall come to pass shall be accomplished, the Messiah will begin to be revealed ... and it will happen at that time that the treasury of manna will come down again from on high and they will eat of it in those years because these are they who have arrived at the consummation of time.

I knew then that the substance I had just consumed from John's hand was the very same manna on which my ancestors had survived for over forty years. The food of angels.

I do not know how long the tears flowed, but they poured forth from my eyes silently, leaving behind a strange clarity and sense of purity. *Yes,* I thought *my name is Paul. Saul of Tarsus lies discarded on this floor like the repellent scales that covered my eyes on the way to Damascus.*

Although I could no longer see the woman, the fragrance that cloaked her lingered. Roses, I decided, although no roses adorned this room. The effect was subtle yet intoxicating.

After several more moments of silence, John nodded in agreement, but his eyes remained closed. I had forgotten he was there until I saw the motion of his head. Clearly, he was nodding as if in agreement with someone speaking to him. Opening his eyes, he glanced at me and then turned toward the back of the room, beckoning me to follow him. Together, we walked out the open door into a courtyard, in which there stood an odd arrangement of sculptures. Or were they trees? I hesitated, uncertain, but it was evident I was to follow him toward the structures.

As I moved closer, I could see that these were neither trees nor sculptures, but a series of painstakingly crafted memorials of some kind. There were small wooden altars before each one, and, as I watched, John knelt at the nearest, for a few minutes, then rose. Wordlessly, he invited me to do the same. Then he moved on to the second and repeated the gesture.

The instant I knelt at the first altar, I was transported to the Jerusalem Temple. I stood in a vast crowd facing the Pretorium. It must have been just before the Passover, as that would explain why everyone stood outside. No Jew would enter the Gentile quarters in that season, lest he become ritually unclean and prohibited from partaking of the Passover feast. I knew that somehow I had been transported to the past and would come to understand what I saw.

The doors of the portico flew open and the Prelate—a Roman governor I did not know—came out, leading another man clothed in a long purple cloak.

"*Ecce homo!*" the governor shouted, placing his hand on the shoulder of the other man who—I could see now—was gravely wounded. He could barely see past the streams of blood that flowed from deep punctures made by his crown of thorns.

"Look!" cried the governor, "I have brought him out to you so you know I find no guilt in this man."

"Hail, King of the Jews!" the crowd shouted back.

From the eastern side of the courtyard came a horrifying cry: "CRUCIFY HIM! CRUCIFY HIM! FREE BARABBAS!" It was Caiaphas, Annas, and their fellow priests and temple guards.

Although it was impossible, I could see their faces quite clearly. Their features were contorted by malevolence and rage. They were consumed by the kind of depravity and bloodlust that would inhabit me in mere months. An abyss of darkness poured from their eyes.

"Take him yourselves and crucify him!" shouted the man I now knew was Pontius Pilate. "I find no guilt in him!"

Caiaphas spoke. "We have a law, and according to that law, no man may make himself out to be the son of God. This Jesus has done so, and he must die for it."

Pilate removed the man to his chambers, but it felt as if I had *become* the Roman governor. I could hear his thoughts as if they were my own. I looked through his eyes at the battered, bloody face of the man called Jesus and felt Pilate's confusion and pain.

You could stop this, I was thinking, now residing in Pilate's anguished mind. *Why don't You strike us all down?*

"Where are you from?" The words burst from my lips as I stood there, gazing on the man who had come to save the human race. I knew where he was from and I think Pilate sensed it, too. But too often we speak when we have no idea what to say.

Jesus regarded Pilate—regarded me—and I sensed sorrow and pity emanating from him. For me, for Pilate, for each one of us. Here he stood, beaten, bleeding, ridiculed, and yet he pitied me? "Do you not speak to me?"

He remained silent.

"Do you not understand that I have the power to release you?" *Ah Pilate, you lie. You know you have no power. You are about to act like the puppet of Caiaphas you are.*

"You would have no power over me if it had not been given to you from above," he said quietly. "The greater sin belongs to those who handed me over to you."

How can any human understand this merciful, loving God?

In desperation, these words erupted: "What shall I do with you?!"

Through his cracked, bloody lips, came the reply. "You must act as it is written."

"How is it written?" My heart was breaking, tearing into infinitesimal pieces. Pilate's grief was the grief of all suffering humanity.

"Moses and the prophets have foretold my suffering and resurrection," he offered calmly. His gaze was steady and he seemed unafraid, despite the trials he had already withstood and the weight of those to come.

Who are you? Pilate wondered again in my head. *No man calmly permits himself to be scourged, spit on, crucified! No MAN.*

There are no words to describe the grief and anguish that overtook me as I was catapulted out of Pontius Pilate's agony. I did not know if only my spirit traveled or my body as well, but that Roman tribune seemed to personify a perverse blend of courage and cowardice. Of wisdom and ignorance. I felt strangely connected to the man, far more so to him than to my fellow Sanhedrin. I fell prostrate to the ground, wholly incapable of holding myself erect. Only then did I come to understand that grief and love are one. Inextricable.

LVII

Each of the nine successive altars contained mysterious, miraculous visions back in time. I was transported through Pontius Pilate's increasingly dangerous and futile attempts to stop the monstrous evil being perpetrated on this wholly innocent man. I was more and more conscious that Annas and Caiaphas were being used by some unseen force. Their shocking denial of the release of Barabbas and their insistence on the crucifixion of Jesus lacked all reason.

His reply to Pontius Pilate resounded in my mind: *You would have no power over me if it had not been given to you from above ... you must act as it is written ....*

I was astounded at Pilate's actions; at the discernment he seemed to have. Here was a Roman pagan, neither circumcised nor schooled in our Laws, to whom was given knowledge of the Lord Most High. This Roman prelate *knew* whom he beheld, even before he formed his question, *What is truth?* He understood that Truth was standing before him—an understanding denied any of the thousands of chosen priests of the Twelve Tribes of Israel. And to the High Priest, Caiaphas.

I watched Jesus pick up that enormous cross, almost seeming to embrace it. And I witnessed his seemingly endless trek to Golgotha. Three times, he fell under the excruciating weight of his burden. I saw a heartrending, silent exchange between Him and His mother, Mary.

As I approached the next holy site, I saw what looked like a bronze serpent carefully affixed to a wooden pole in front of the altar. *Ah, Lord ... this, I understand!* By the age of five, all Jewish boys have heard about the constant complaining of our people as they wandered in the desert for forty years. The punishment of the snakes is the stuff of nightmares. Very few of us whine or complain about our own lives after we learn that story.

As I drew closer, the fragrance of roses was so powerful that I stopped and looked all around for a profusion of rose bushes. What I saw was Her ... prostrate on the ground in front of this clearly holy site. I realized it was not a serpent I'd seen from afar, but instead, the carefully crafted figure of a man. A crucified man. She had shaped a bronze image of her Son dying on the cross.

The mother of Jesus rose in one fluid motion and started to walk toward me. Although the shadows were beginning to lengthen and dusk approached, I could clearly see her expression, the luminosity of those extraordinary eyes. Her gaze was indescribably compelling, drawing me in with an intensity I had never experienced. Everything around me faded into nothingness. My mind, which should have been filled with a thousand questions, was wholly blank. Just as her outstretched hand touched my cloak, I heard the sound of intense winds and was enveloped in what I can only describe as some type of fiery conveyance that carried me to a place I knew did not exist on earth.

The knowledge, understanding, and wisdom I have shared in my writing over these past thirty years were infused within me there, in the fourth level of the heavens. Carried there on the wings of a cloud, I witnessed splendors and glory, which cannot be described with any accuracy or precision, for much of what I experienced in that place cannot fit into any language, at least none that I know. My attempts to do so sound fanciful, even to my own ears. But I will briefly tell you about the light, the place, and the Being who led me to the Lord.

We know and understand light as a thing that surrounds us and which we perceive in contrast with darkness and shadow. But in this place, the light was not external; it suffused everything there.

The brightness of the light was so intense and pervasive, it should have burned my eyes and scorched my skin. Instead, it seemed to merge with the air. As I breathed in, it was as if I swallowed the light until I, too, was translucent, like everything I saw in that place of endless glories. There were birds with dazzling plumage, none the same as any other. There were grasslands, rivers, and lakes in which the trees and the waters sang—yes, sang—the praises of the Lord.

The celestial being who greeted and led me up through incandescent mists was gigantic. It was composed of fire and light, and I could see its face only when it bent over to speak to me, which it did only once because the first time I heard it, I fell forward and prostrated myself before it, sure I was hearing the voice of God. The being picked me up as if I were a small child and placed me on my feet, pointing upward into the mists.

"This is the Triune God. He is who you adore."

I have only a vague memory of seeing the Lord Himself. Dimly, in my mind's eye, I can see the shimmering, purely white image of an immense lamb like that I knew to have been provided to Abraham for the sacrifice that saved Isaac. Again, I fell forward, flattening myself before Him. I heard His voice again.

"I am true food and true drink, the Bread of Life. I am the manna, the food of angels on which your ancestors fed for forty years. It is through me that humanity is granted eternal life. Go and tell them how much the Father and I love them; explain that all that I did is for the salvation of each precious human soul. With my death, I conquered the Adversary. I am the truth, the way, and the life."

It was thus that I was schooled in the impenetrable wisdom, knowledge, and counsel of His spirit. I do not know how long I stayed in the fourth heaven. I think it was many weeks because when I was returned to Ephesus, my beard evidenced two months' growth. It was there, in Ephesus, that I began to put into words what I was given.

I am immensely grateful to Aurelius for being with me during my last night on earth, and for this final opportunity to describe the depth of the riches and wisdom and knowledge of the Lord. Had it not been for his insistence, this letter would never have been written. How inscrutable are God's judgments and how unknowable his ways!

For from him and through him are all things. To God, be glory forever.

For he himself is our peace, who has made the two groups one and has destroyed the barrier, the dividing wall of hostility, by setting aside in his flesh the law with its commands and regulations. His purpose was to create in himself one new humanity out of the two, thus making peace, and in one body to reconcile both of them to God through the cross, by which he put to death their hostility. He came and preached peace to you who were far away and peace to those who were near. For through him we both have access to the Father by one Spirit.

Consequently, you are no longer foreigners and strangers, but fellow citizens with God's people and also members of His household, built on the foundation of the apostles and prophets, with Christ Jesus himself as the chief cornerstone. In Him, the whole building is joined together and rises to become a holy temple in the Lord. And in Him, you, too, are being built together to become a dwelling in which God lives by his Spirit.

LVIII

AURELIUS

Mamertine Prison, Rome

Paul's last chapter was cut short. Precisely as he completed that magnificent hymn, which had clearly been dictated to him by Our Lord, the sunrise appeared. Shortly after that came Aberkios, the executioner.

Paul smiled at him, and it crossed my mind that this might have been the first smile the man had witnessed in … how long? I can tell you that the radiance from that smile suffused the dark, damp cell with such light and heat that the executioner looked puzzled. "Did you men have some kind of a fire in here?" he muttered, blinking.

I had put the chains back on Paul, both of us feeling compelled to continue the ruse, but they caused him no trouble as he eagerly followed Aberkios into the courtyard. Lifting his face to the sky, he whispered something. At first, I thought he was responding to the feeling of the sun after close to two years in the dark—but as I hurried to catch up, I heard him say, "Lord, how well you know I am nothing. That I have existed these sixty-plus years has been solely due to You … to Your unfathomable will. For everything—all who draw breath, even the stones I walk on—have their being in You. I give thanks for the suffering endured for Your glory, and for your forgiveness …

for the conviction that I go now to see Stephen, Abigahil, and all who live in Your household. I praise You, Lord of the Universe!"

By the time he finished his prayer, he was standing at the stake, staring at his executioner as if willing him to pick up the rod and tear open the maze of scars on his back.

Aberkios looked fixedly at Paul, his mouth agape, tears coursing down his ravaged face. Paul extended his gnarled, arthritic fingers and blessed the man, and as he did so, his beatific smile grew wider. "This is your last act for the demon," he said quietly, "but it is one you must complete. Our Lord has ordained it so."

Aberkios, God bless him, led Paul away from the stake, refusing to inflict the forty blows allotted to Roman criminals. He signaled him to kneel and lay his upper body on the blood-stained bench. Ignoring the torrent of tears flowing down his own face, Aberkios raised his blade … and it was done.

EPILOGUE

AURELIUS
Corinth, Greece

It has been five years since that last night of Paul's life. Each Sunday, I am asked by Priscilla and Acquila, the leaders of the church at Corinth, to read Paul's final letter before beginning our worship service. It does my heart good to have an audience for these words at last.

Upon leaving Rome and moving to Corinth, I fulfilled my promise to Paul and married. My wife's name is Hannah— yes, the same as that of Paul's own. Hannah had heard Paul's speeches when first he came to Corinth and was baptized by him soon after. As one of his first disciples here, she'd brought her entire family to hear him, and all are now followers of the Way.

I met her the week I arrived. Dazed and sorrowful from the loss of the great man and of my identity as a legionary, I was feeling a more profound sense of loneliness than I had ever before endured. I had expected to feel sad, to grieve, but this? This awful gnawing hole in my gut and heart? I could not sleep or eat. I could not even weep.

I had been wandering through the agora in Corinth when she approached me where I stood, forlorn in my dusty, unkempt legionary uniform. I'd stopped in front of a vendor, trying to decide whether to buy some dates, but my mind was consumed with how foolish I felt. How cowardly. I now detested all that the Roman Legion stood for—could no longer be a soldier, having deserted my post—but I had not been able to bear the final indignation of donning civilian clothes for the first time in fourteen years. I think part of me hoped to be identified as a deserter by one of my former comrades passing by and punished accordingly.

"You look lost."

I looked up at the young woman before me, surprised that she spoke Latin and immediately aware that her observation was not meant to refer to geography.

Yes, I thought, *I am most assuredly lost, and more. I am bereft. Aimless and adrift.*

"My name is Hannah," said the girl, "and yours?" Her smile was dimpled and winning, her lovely blue eyes vibrant.

Hannah? Her name is Hannah?

She appeared so confident, so serene, I was momentarily mute. She seemed to exude a kind of joy I knew I could never match. This was no time to get teary-eyed, but that name ... the heartbreak it conjured in me was more than I could bear. I felt the tears leach from my eyes as I beheld this astounding woman who wore the name of Paul's dead wife.

Instantly, her smile faded, and her beautiful eyes clouded. Solemnly, she reached out to grab my hand in hers, which was as soft as a baby lamb. "Something horrible has happened to you," she said quietly. "I am so sorry. Will you come with me so that I can make you some tea? Perhaps you can tell me what troubles you so."

It was an audacious overture and yet, somehow, exactly right. Obediently, I followed Hannah down the adjacent alley, which led to another and then a third. *I will never find my way back through this warren,* I thought. After a sudden right, we stopped in front of a large walled home with a bright blue door. Hannah swiftly opened it and beckoned me into a generous courtyard.

Before I followed her inside, I hesitated. "Hannah, why are you so trusting of me, a perfect stranger?" She turned and walked back onto the street to look up at me, her lovely face grave.

"You are no stranger to me. I have seen you in my dreams for many months. I knew you would come here to Corinth—to me." She seemed to be waiting for a reply to her guileless, almost child-like declaration, but I could only regard her in utter bafflement as she turned to walk through the door of the courtyard. Over her shoulder, she added, "Please do not be afraid."

What else could I do but follow?

A distinguished-looking older couple sat under a copse of olive, cypress, and laurel trees. Both rose at our entry, smiling curiously first at Hannah and then at me.

"Aurelius," said Hannah, though I didn't remember having told her my name, "these are my parents, Patryk and Aurora."

"Hello. Welcome, Aurelius. Please have a seat," said Patryk, waving his hand at a cushioned couch under a cypress tree. His expression continued to exude benign curiosity.

Hannah's mother—the image of Hannah plus several decades—disappeared with her daughter into the house, presumably to prepare the tea.

After a moment or two, Patryk decided to fill the silence that had fallen between us. "Since there are no legionnaire barracks in Corinth, and you look as if it has been some time since you have enjoyed the benefits of such accommodations, I assume that you are no longer a soldier?"

Regarding him steadily, I realized I was no longer

ashamed of what I had done. In fact, I was proud. Nero's insanity, the corruption of his regime, the disregard for all that is considered good and right by most of the top officers in the Legion, bubbled up to the surface of my mind, along with a thousand images of courageous men who had died on the blood-soaked battlefields for a Rome that no longer existed. Maybe it never had. I felt free for the first time in many years.

I smiled wryly at my host. "You are correct, sir. Rome would describe me as a deserter, although I served loyally for fourteen years." Shrugging, I pointed at my dusty, no-longer-white tunic and stained scarlet cloak. "I apologize for my appearance, but I have no other clothes than these—and wasn't expecting to be meeting anyone."

Just then, Hannah and her mother returned with brimming trays of late summer vegetables, cheeses, olives, figs, and bread. There was no tea, but one of the plates included a large jug of wine and two goblets.

Patryk filled the cups with wine, handed me one, and said, "I can only imagine what might have brought a former legionnaire to Corinth, Aurelius. If you care to tell me your story, I would like to hear it."

I caught Hannah looking over her shoulder at me as she disappeared back into the house. She was smiling that adorably dimpled smile. I was coming to feel that she was the most beautiful woman I had ever seen. When her father caught my gaze of open admiration, the heat rose in my cheeks. "Sir, I—"

Thankfully, he cut off whatever it was I might have offered in defense of my boldness. "Aurelius, please call me Patryk. I want you to know that I understand your … feelings. Hannah is the image of her mother, and I well remember being struck by that pellucid beauty years ago. These women … there is transparency to them. It is as if you can see right to the bottom of their souls."

I was honestly astounded at the accuracy of Patryk's description. I had known many women in my travels, but it hadn't taken me long to see that Hannah was unique. For the entire thirty-minute walk from the agora to her home, though she must have been curious about my circumstances, she had been content with silence. She had merely walked by my side as if she had been doing so for a very long time.

Pellucidus ... so clear the light shines through. Yes, that is completely fitting for you, lovely Hannah.

Patryk's Latin, like that of his daughter, was flawless. Without thinking, I said, "I thank you for opening your home to a perfect stranger—an ex-Roman soldier, no less." What I wanted to add but didn't was, *particularly when it is clear that I have no means of taking care of your daughter.*

Patryk regarded me steadily. "Aurelius, I welcome you here because Hannah brought you home. Never before has she done such a thing. She recognizes you."

Recognizes me? What a strange comment, and yet I felt I understood what he meant. The reality was taking root in me by the second: This woman and I were destined for each other.

We talked into the dawn, Patryk and I. Sometime after my third generous chalice of wine, I reached into my satchel and pulled out the scroll that would become this book and offered it to him. After reading just the first few chapters, he jumped to his feet and asked if he could take it to Priscilla and Aquila, leaders of the Corinth church. When I assented, he asked if I would accompany him.

"Sir, I am not dressed for such a meeting ...."

Patryk frowned. "Of course, Aurelius! Please forgive my thoughtlessness! I will accompany you to their home later in this new day. First, let us get you a bath, fresh clothes, and some rest."

As if conjured by his comments, a slim young man appeared.

Patryk stood and said, "Aurelius, follow me up to the roof where our servant Giougius will draw a warm bath for you and provide fresh clothes. He will then show you to your room, where you must feel free to sleep as long as you like."

After several hours of good rest, I changed into one of Patryk's tunics and joined him once again in the courtyard. After exchanging a few pleasantries, he and I walked rapidly back down the streets that Hannah had led me through the evening before.

"Hannah is different from her sisters," Patryk said as we reached and passed the agora where I had met Hannah. "While they had no interest in studying the philosophers, Hannah took to the Dialogues as if born to scholarly work." He stopped suddenly in front of the Temple of Athena and looked over at the beautiful façade. "In fact," he continued, "by the time Hannah was fourteen, she told us that Plato was correct. There is just one God, Logos. Prayers to these gods and goddesses in the form of humans were of no avail. Needless to say, Aurora and I were unsurprised when Hannah told us that she had become a Christian following her hearing Paul speak, there—at the Tomb of the Unknown God."

I followed his gaze to a large stone slab with writing I could not read.

"The following day, her sisters and we came to listen to Paul and were baptized as well." Patryk turned back and looked quietly at me for a few moments. We were almost the same height, and our gazes met squarely. I felt immense gratitude for this patrician Greek man and was surprised to realize that I felt no discomfort while he stood silently probing me.

"Priscilla and Acquila live just over there, Aurelius. They were wonderfully close friends of Paul's and will insist that you stay with them for several days. In addition to reading and discussing this last letter, they will want to hear about everything he said during your time with him. You can help them resolve their grief at his loss. I would advise you to accept their hospitality, and perhaps while you are with them, you will be moved to become a member of the church. Does this sound reasonable to you, my son, or do I overstep myself?" Smiling wryly, he added, "Perhaps I am being ... too fatherly?"

"Patryk, I welcome your direction. Before I met Hannah—and then you—I was aimless and grief-stricken ... more confused than I had ever been. Quite miraculously, I now feel as if I have stepped into the rest of my life." I paused to take in his quiet smile, then added, "Patryk, I never knew my father. He died in battle before I was born. So ... I suppose I am not really sure what *too fatherly* might mean."

"Good," he replied as if something important had been decided. "Before Priscilla and Acquila scoop you up, let me explain what I meant earlier when I told you that Hannah had *recognized* you. My daughter has had extraordinarily detailed dreams for quite a long time—about you and Paul at the prison in Rome, his execution, and your arrival in Corinth. She has also dreamed of your marriage."

Pretending to ignore the flush in my cheeks and clearly expecting no response to this extraordinary revelation, he led me over to meet Priscilla and Acquila. As he'd predicted—I ended up staying with them for almost a week.

Hannah and I married and are parents now, of two spirited boys: four-year-old Paul and two-year-old David. Each morning, before we begin our day, the four of us offer thanks to God for His profligate blessings. Until the end of my days, I shall work to be grateful for each earthly moment, for I recall Paul's grief at the perfunctory way that he had said good-bye to his wife and son, secure in the knowledge that they would be back together in just a few hours.

Perhaps, dear reader, these last words of Paul have surprised or even shocked you. Perchance you continue to wonder at the improbability of a murderer of Christians being used by the Lord as his last apostle. No less did Paul. After thirty years of risking his life for Christ, he remained convinced that none of his actions could be explained or justified by any other than the Lord. To his last breath, Paul believed that all of His creatures—the very worst and the very best of us—can be used by Christ in the mysterious, miraculous economy of salvation.

Of the many works published about the life and times of St. Paul, these are among those I found most helpful:

Rabban Gamaliel by Ralph Harvey, published by Kindle Books, 2005.

Stoic Six Pack 9: The PreSocratics by Benjamin Cocker, George Grote, and WA Heidel, published by Enhanced Media, 2016.

Paul: A Biography, by N.T.Wright, published by Harper One (London), 2017.

Paul of Tarsus: A Visionary Life, by Edward Stourton, published by Paulist Press, 2004.

The Jew of Tarsus: An Unorthodox Portrait of Paul, by Hugh Schonfield, published by McDonald and Co. (London), 1946.

The Babylonian Talmud, by Isidore Epstein, published by BN Publishing, 2006.

Rabban Gamaliel II: The Legal Traditions, by Shamai Kanter, published by Brown University Brown Judaic Studies, 1980.

Rabban Gamaliel Ben Simeon, by Solomon Sadowsky, published by Hebrew Publishing Company, 1941.

The Trial of Socrates, by I.F. Stone, published by Little Brown and Company, 1988.

Imperium: A Novel of Ancient Rome, by Robert Harris, published by Simon and Schuster, 2006.

Jesus and the Jewish Roots of the Eucharist, by Brant Pitre, published by Doubleday, 2011.

Gates of Fire by Steven Pressfield, published by Doubleday, 1998.

Paul, the Apostle of Christ, (film), directed by Andrew Hyatt, 2018.

Writing is always an audacious act. While our spoken words fade, our written ones endure. Writing fiction is even more bold, particularly when the subjects of the novels are known to have existed—as Pontius Pilate and Saul of Tarsus are. Many have strong opinions about these people, positive or negative. Records of their actions have been handed down to us to be studied and debated. A variety of motives for their efforts have been imagined by those who have studied them. But in the end, whether writing fiction or nonfiction, we conjure up these people. We assemble the few known facts about their lives and weave them into a coherent—we hope plausible—story.

Throughout the writing of this book, my decision to imagine the early life of St. Paul has seemed alternatively foolish and wise, arrogant and humbling … and a panoply of other feelings as paradoxical as Paul himself. Of one thing I am sure, however. After a year of immersing myself in the life of the young man called Saul, I am convinced that he is a man for our times. I undertook this book for many reasons, but primarily because I came to see Saul as a man who had no interest in sidestepping the meaning of things, or in appeasing hurt feelings or bruised consciences. Saul was interested in just one thing: truth. Whether it was the truth about the God he chased for the first part of his life or the God he died for, or about himself, Saul permitted no margin of error. Saul lacked any tolerance for artifice or mitigation. And, upon learning the depths of his early arrogance and transgression, he spent the rest of his life risking it for the Christ he had persecuted. As I said … he is a man for our times.

Like most of my novels, *My Name is Saul* was not my idea. Many writers talk about the sources of their inspiration.

They often insist, with natural wonder, that their characters present themselves and take on lives of their own, seemingly outside of their control. These are not all "believers," by any means— and yet many assert that writing fiction includes a dimension that can only be called *mystical*. Indeed this is true for me.

Upon completing my last novel, I was stunned to "hear" that my next book would be about St. Paul ... Apostle of the Apostles. On more than one occasion, I complained to my husband that this was one of the most foolhardy efforts I had ever taken on. I could only console myself with the fact that it was not my idea but Someone Else's.

As I sat reeling from the implanted idea and began to research Saul of Tarsus, I grew more and more enthusiastic ... excited, even. Perhaps I could penetrate the obscurity with which the early life of St. Paul is shrouded. How could I manage such a task? Because, as I continued to study, search, think, I realized that Saul of Tarsus is a man I *get*.

Get as in, *AHA! I know what certainty tastes like, and Saul of Tarsus was a man of certainty.*

The array of intellectual and financial gifts given Saul of Tarsus was prodigious. Although very little is known about his early life (precisely why I wanted to start there in this story), most scholars agree that he came from a wealthy family and received extensive private tutoring. Paul himself wrote that he had been a student of Gamaliel at the Jerusalem Temple.

The young Saul took to religious scholarship as naturally as does any prodigy, and soon became known as the most zealous of the Pharisees. Think about that for a moment. The Pharisees wielded the most power among the seventy-member Jerusalem Religious Council—the Sanhedrin—and Saul sat among them.

Before he reached the age of thirty!

As he told it, he became the most feared persecutor of the followers of the Way—the Christians—until he was quite literally toppled from his throne of certitude. At that point, he became ... drum roll here ... the Apostle to the Gentiles, trading his Jewish *Saul,* for the Roman *Paul.*

Certainties are so seductive, are they not? Whether about religion, the Bible, the hypocrisy of Christians, or the broader concerns of politics, many of our certainties loom so large that they eclipse everything else—including the truth standing right in front of us.

Moving on to the particulars of my story: Is there any historical evidence of Saul's marriage? Not as such, but neither is there any evidence to the contrary. Israeli men—even rabbis and high priests—were expected to marry by the age of eighteen. If they were not married by twenty, it was cause for concern. Since there are extensive gaps in our knowledge of Saul's early life, indeed, such a union is at least possible, if not probable.

As for some of the other imaginings set forth here: Saul's dream of celibacy is my fiction. Only among the Essenes would celibacy have been revered. For a Pharisee like Saul, the ascetic philosophy of the Essenes was not likely to have been at all attractive.

Most scholars agree that Saul was not in Jerusalem during the crucifixion; that he was most likely in Tarsus at the time.

My information about his family and business was gleaned from the work of scriptural scholars, as were the time and place of his death.

The events of the weeks and years after Paul's dramatic conversion are a source of controversy—even in the Bible itself. In one section of Luke's Book of Acts, we read that Paul began preaching about Christ immediately after his healing. In another chapter, we see that he traveled to Arabia and spent several years there, leaving only when the Apostle Barnabus came to collect him in Tarsus.

It is the latter explanation—that he spent several years in Arabia before setting out to preach—that fits my understanding of the man. Moving from his rage and wish to kill and maim the people of the Way to proclaiming the truth of Christ in under a week seems unreasonable, does it not? I imagine that for any man, even Paul, a period of many weeks or even years would be essential for healing.

And what of his time in Ephesus with John and Mary? From almost the beginning of writing Saul's story, while pondering the words of those who have studied him, Ephesus seemed the most reasonable source of his profound mystical revelations. I never questioned it.

Because Saul would have known the Torah and Prophets so intimately, he thought and spoke in their language. As such, many of Paul's words and thoughts are taken directly from the Bible. (In a few of those direct quotations, I altered names and places to suit my story, but the essence remains.)

It has been a distinct privilege to insinuate myself into the early life of this man named Saul. As I wrote, some episodes felt too brutal—too raw—to render in words, but I was impelled to do so in spite of myself. I hope I have done these moments justice, as they are integral to revealing the truth of the man who came to be known as the first theologian.

A PREVIEW OF LIN WILDER'S

Plausible Liars
A Dr. Lindsey McCall Medical Mystery
Coming in 2021

"Dr. McCall, you were convicted of intentional murder and for two years were incarcerated in a Texas prison, losing your license to practice medicine and your position as Cardiologist at the University of Houston Medical School, isn't that correct?"

Lindsey was prepared for the questions. Of course, the San Francisco District Attorney would bring up her two-year prison term in the infamous Huntsville Prison. And would omit the facts that Lindsey was acquitted, her license restored and was offered the Chief of Cardiology position at the medical school. Brownmiller would have been a fool not to lead with the salacious questions, and the DA was no fool.

Before she could reply, Zach Cunningham was on his feet, shouting, "OBJECTION! D.A. Brownmiller's question is not only irrelevant to this case, but it impugns Dr. McCall's character and the testimony that Dr. McCall has sworn to provide this court. Further, Judge, in closed session with you just yesterday, Ms. Brownmiller agreed to limit the scope of this case, and—"

Before Zach could say another word, Sandra Brownmiller sprang to her stiletto-shod feet and launched a torrent of additional volleys at Cunningham, until the Judge was moved to bang her gavel and shout, "Both of you, in my chambers, NOW!"

The two attorneys made an odd pair as they dutifully followed the judge out of the courtroom. Sandra Brownmiller was six feet tall, and in her heels, she rose another four inches. She was a handsome woman, not pretty as such, but with her long red hair and stature, she commanded attention.

Zach Cunningham, the law partner of Lindsey's husband Rich, was five-foot-five, and his recently regrown dreadlocks rhythmically flapped against his gray suit as he exited the courtroom. The ragged white scar that began at his right eyebrow and extended across his cheek traversed his ebony face and made his unusual features memorable.

The courtroom suddenly quiet, Lindsey sat thinking about how the monumental fiasco had begun, close to a year earlier. It had all started when she and Rich accepted an invitation to spend the weekend in Palo Alto with their good friends, Dr. Steve Cooper and his wife, Kate Townsend. After dinner Saturday evening, the four sat relaxing on the couple's beautifully decorated patio, listening to the contented sounds of Steve and Kate's two sleeping children through the baby monitor. In the course of their idle conversation, Kate asked Lindsey about gender dysphoria.

Lindsey, who had been pondering a nagging problem that had come up in her animal research lab, didn't hear Kate's question at first.

"Honey," Rich said gently, waving his can of Grolsch beer in front of her face, "Kate's asking you something."

Kate, who was an investigative journalist for the *Houston Tribune* though she lived in northern California, explained that their four-year-old son was in pre-school with a boy and girl who had been diagnosed with gender dysphoria by a leading California pediatric psychologist. Her interest piqued, she'd embarked on a series for the paper with the working title, "Creating Chemical Eunuchs: Androgynizing America's Children."

What did Lindsey think about the subject?

Groaning inwardly, Rich tipped his beer and consumed what remained of it in a gulp. *These last ten months have been perfect. No kidnappings. No threats to the world. Life on the central coast of California has been calm, peaceful, predictable. Kate Townsend, need I tell you how much I will miss these wonderfully boring days?*